KENNETH GILES
Murder Pluperfect

WALKER AND COMPANY · NEW YORK

Copyright © 1970 by Kenneth Giles

All rights reserved. No part of this book may be
reproduced or transmitted in any form or by any
means, electric or mechanical, including photocopying,
recording, or by any information storage and retrieval
system, without permission in writing from the Publisher.

All the characters and events portrayed in this story
are fictitious.

First published in the United States of America
in 1970 by the Walker Publishing Company, Inc.

This paperback edition first published in 1984.

ISBN: 0-8027-3094-9

Library of Congress Catalog Card Number: 71-120402

Printed in the United States of America

10 9 8 7 6 5 4 3 2 1

Murder Pluperfect

Harry's watch read eight forty-five as the red telephone rang.

The Colonel's mottled hand took the handset up. He listened. Rattled, read Harry, but the unflappable type at bottom. "All right, carry on." The Chief Constable hung up.

"Good man, my Superintendent on murder, not that we have half a case a year, rest of the time he is on other duties. Gerald Snape found dead, knife through his heart, plumb centre, by the early morning cleaner in his office at Little Brittox, that's near the Cathedral. You saw him after our telephone conversation yesterday?"

"Half an hour. I thought he was all you said. A sly fellow on the cruel cat-and-mouse side."

"The body is cooling. The Super used a thermometer. I'd trust him more than the surgeon, a youngish fellow. Super says death was between nine and nine thirty last night."

"He narrows it," said Harry, perhaps a bit sourly.

"He spent fifteen years in D Division before he swapped down here. Knows his onions, or cadavers if you prefer."

"Weapon?"

"Cheap kitchen knife, mass-produced for fancy French cooks who read magazines. New, he thought, and therefore with a good edge. It being a stuffy old night he was in a white broadcloth shirt, of the old cricketing type but better than synthetic for drinking up the sweat, and St Michael slacks."

"I don't think he was the kind of man who wore informal clothes on formal occasions," grunted Harry. "A semi-off-record gathering, one thinks."

Other titles in the Walker British Mystery Series

Peter Alding • MURDER IS SUSPECTED
Peter Alding • RANSOM TOWN
Jeffrey Ashford • SLOW DOWN THE WORLD
Jeffrey Ashford • THREE LAYERS OF GUILT
Pierre Audemars • NOW DEAD IS ANY MAN
Marion Babson • DANGEROUS TO KNOW
Marion Babson • THE LORD MAYOR OF DEATH
Brian Ball • MONTENEGRIN GOLD
Josephine Bell • A QUESTION OF INHERITANCE
Josephine Bell • TREACHERY IN TYPE
Josephine Bell • VICTIM
W. J. Burley • DEATH IN WILLOW PATTERN
W. J. Burley • TO KILL A CAT
Desmond Cory • THE NIGHT HAWK
Desmond Cory • UNDERTOW
John Creasey • THE BARON AND THE UNFINISHED PORTRAIT
John Creasey • HELP FROM THE BARON
John Creasey • THE TOFF AND THE FALLEN ANGELS
John Creasey • TRAP THE BARON
June Drummond • FUNERAL URN
June Drummond • SLOWLY THE POISON
William Haggard • THE NOTCH ON THE KNIFE
William Haggard • THE POISON PEOPLE
William Haggard • TOO MANY ENEMIES
William Haggard • VISA TO LIMBO
William Haggard • YESTERDAY'S ENEMY
Simon Harvester • MOSCOW ROAD
Simon Harvester • ZION ROAD
J. G. Jeffreys • SUICIDE MOST FOUL
J. G. Jeffreys • A WICKED WAY TO DIE
J. G. Jeffreys • THE WILFUL LADY
Elizabeth Lemarchand • CHANGE FOR THE WORSE
Elizabeth Lemarchand • STEP IN THE DARK
Elizabeth Lemarchand • SUDDENLY WHILE GARDENING
Elizabeth Lemarchand • UNHAPPY RETURNS
Laurie Mantell • A MURDER OR THREE
John Sladek • BLACK AURA
John Sladek • INVISIBLE GREEN

I

HARRY JAMES HAD got his step to Chief Inspector, entailing several lunches with the hierarchy and a return cocktail party which he could not afford. Any satisfaction was dispelled by a grinning civilian accountant who informed him that his rank and salary increase would come into effect after he had cleaned up his arrears of leave, amounting to sixteen days.

"Have a good break, Mr James."

It so happened that the Inspector possessed a wife and three children, and a heavy mortgage on a small house. His wife was not the kind of woman to spend her holidays at home, whatever appeal was made, and the new Chief Inspector flinched at the thought of more borrowing. On this particular late August morning he was seated at the overcrowded desk in his small cubicle of a room when the door opened and the sardonic face of Superintendent Hawker peered round.

"Come in, sir," said Harry getting to his feet. He had had a grouch against Hawker over the past year.

"They say Italy is very pleasant at this time of the year and, my, how they dote on toddlers there," observed Hawker.

"You are throwing my poverty in my face like the sadistic old party you are! It'll have to be an unpleasant relative of mine who has an old house at Clacton where she lets rooms."

"Trust yourself to God and my benevolence," said the old Super. "Do you know Colonel Angel?"

"Never met him. Chief Constable of Greymouth, isn't he?"

"The same. He asked me if I knew a bright young man. I said no, but that you might be better than nothing. A 'cottage' with four bedrooms and twenty-five nicker a week for light gentlemanly work."

"Such as?" In spite of his current feelings for Hawker Harry was impressed.

"Investigating a murder."

"It's my wife who is addicted to funny programmes and one must say we both like them non-malicious."

"It happened in 1874," said Hawker slowly and deadpan.

"Good heavens!"

"One of the Chief Constable's friends is a local millionaire, Sir Charles Fennel, a man in his early sixties. His great-aunt, Penelope Fennel, had a fiancé who died of tartar emetic in 1874. The circumstances were mysterious and they gave the poor lady a ghastly time at the inquest. Nobody was ever brought to trial and she broke her neck out hunting two years later. It might have been suicide, because she had started to ride like a madwoman. Anyway Sir Charles wants a pro eye cast over it. If you can make out a case, he'll hire somebody to write a book. Gawd, we do the work and all the literary bums reef the royalties from the sweat of our brow! We should have a statutory fee on each book sold."

"I'll take it sight unseen," said Harry, "anything except Clacton. However, there is so much research involved that I'd just dent the surface, no real digging possible in that time."

"I said he is a millionaire," said Hawker with a hint of irritation. "He went to the best research organisation there is. They provided photostats of everything written on the case. Then, of course, he approached old Angel for the police end of it and he climbed upstairs to us. Now Sir Charles displaces a lot of financial water. It was agreed to provide you, or whoever could do the job, with the confidential files, on condition that nothing from them was directly quoted without written permission from the Home Office." He shrugged and got up. "I gather that Sir Charles has a wife," he said cryptically before leaving.

The Inspector took the lift to the reference library, and took down *Who's Who*. The entry read:

Fennel, Charles Edward C.B.E., cr. 1959, D.S.O.: s. of the late William and Mary Fennel: industrialist and banker: represented Greymouth in the Conservative Interest 1950-1960: educated Eton and Oxford: hobbies, reading, the theatre: m., 1948, Gertrude, d. of the late Mr and Mrs Edward Humphrey: 1 son: residence, Greymouth Manor, Sussex.

One of those typical, understated entries, he thought. It was curious the way people reacted. Some famous men doled out a few essential facts: others, mediocre, could fill a column with trumpery triumphs. He would have to try elsewhere.

It was a serene, warm morning and he sweated slightly as his taxi ground through heavy traffic to Fleet Street. He spent half an hour in a newspaper library to which he had the entrée. From the cuts, Sir Charles Fennel was a big, rather hulking fellow with a mop of hair and a heavy moustache. He had won his D.S.O. in 1940, being wounded fairly severely in the process. As an M.P. he had been a Churchill worshipper and later pro-Suez. "Millionaire industrialist and banker" was the phrase often used. He occasionally rated a gossip paragraph as a buyer of rare books and as a benefactor of various theatre trusts. Otherwise his life really seemed devoid of newsworthy incident.

The Inspector telephoned his wife, who was harassed but pleased and pestered him with detailed questions about suitable clothes until a distant infant howling cut the conversation short. Then by bus to the City and a broker friend.

"Pity you didn't hang on to those shares," said the broker mechanically, "instead of selling at such a low ebb."

"Do you know anybody who would buy three kids?"

"I'm a bear in that market myself," sighed his friend.

"About Sir Charles Fennel, Jim, what do you know?"

"Fennel!" The broker was stung.

"Now, now, he's Simon Pure in the original so far as I know. It's only that he has asked me, while on holiday, to do some research for him and I like to know what manner of bloke I'm working for."

They had known each other too long for the broker to question further. Instead he summoned two cups of coffee.

"Great big fellow personally, racially Highland Celt so I understand, though the Fennels came south in the late seventeenth century. Taciturn sort of chap: not a clubbable man at all, in fact I do not think he belongs to one. Likes cricket though and riding, I happen to know that from a friend who used to live near him. He's got an eighteenth-century manor in Dorset. As for business, he is the fourth Fennel of great note. The original gentleman from the Heelands became a prosperous ironfounder, his son manufactured steam engines and in the seventies and eighties added pure finance to the stable. Then came our present chap's father who merged, consolidated, got huge 1914-18 contracts but drew his horns in before the 1920 slump. He died in 1950, by which time the family business was what our American friends call a conglomerate. The present incumbent was among the first to get into general electronics, computers and office machinery. Food processing is another activity. He is on the board of a bank. A man of good judgment—it is bred in him—and conservative financially. The only thing he ever quotes is Wellington to the effect that the General with most reserves always wins, so he is miserly with dividends, which does not precisely endear him to the shareholders. Oh! He has a son at Harvard."

"Thanks, old boy." Inspector James left him to it. Looking at his watch, he saw that it was noon. In half an hour he had to be in Eastcheap to meet his factotum, one Sergeant Cedric Honeybody, in a matter of a gentleman who cashed forged travellers' cheques ostensibly drawn upon a German bank. Cupidity and reverence for the mark being what it was, it was easy for this ersatz traveller to pretend he had run out of money and to be in such a confused state that he gladly gave the astute publican twenty per cent discount in changing fifty pounds' worth. By dint of placing little flags upon a map of London the Inspector had espied a certain pattern in the campaign, the supposition being that in ten days' time the Eastcheap region might be hit. Sergeant Honeybody, whom Nature had designed for such assignments, had been delegated to approach the licensees of the more prosperous pubs and implore them to keep the man in conversation while some satrap dialled a certain number. He looked like making this a life's work, upon expenses, it being the accepted rule that on such jobs one must drink a bit, and Harry had arranged to meet him in a popular establishment called the Old Grey Mare.

The Sergeant, the hatching in his size eighteen neck readily recognisable from behind, was the life and soul of a party at the bar. He nevertheless saw his superior officer out of the corner of his eye. Harry went to the snack-bar section and ordered hors-d'oeuvres and bottled ale. He read the midday paper until Honeybody joined him.

The Sergeant was wearing a check suit and looked like a possibly dishonest bookie. "'Allo, 'allo," he said as he took the next stool. "Another eight bungs signed on, leaving six to go. Good work, Honeybody, did I hear you say?"

"No," said the Inspector tolerantly. Over the years a certain camaraderie had grown up between them.

"Having had lamb chops baked in egg and breadcrumbs at the last shop, I'll just skirmish with a bit of the veal and ham pie and a pint of best bitter."

For himself, after completing his first course, the Inspector ordered cold roast beef and salad. The trouble was that the higher in rank you got, the more difficult it was to eat at the public expense. As a Chief Inspector his opportunities to save a little in this way would become scarcer. He vowed that before he left on holiday he would find some excuse—say, those hotel robberies—for a memorable meal indeed.

". . . holidays." He had not been listening to the Sergeant.

"Eh?"

"Your name is on the holiday list beginning Sunday."

"I've got to take accrued leave at Inspector's pay before taking the step-up."

"One day we'll all go on strike," said the Sergeant, "and when the mean bastards are cowerin' in the coal cellars of the House of Commons with the mob baying outside under the lamp-posts they'll wish they never begrudged us a few bob."

"Have you been drinking?"

"Only in the line of duty."

"Watch that particular line when I'm away: you might be assigned to somebody who doesn't like your signals."

"There's a lot in that: I'd thought of it. Where are you going?"

"I've had a peculiar offer relayed per old Hawker but it's a godsend financially."

"Watch it, Harry. It's my turn for advice. He's up to something."

"I can't think what. I'll tell you about it."

Honeybody listened, then said, "I was considering taking my own leave as it's getting late in the year. Would you okay my two weeks at the same time?"

"It might be a good solution," said the Inspector.

"Another thing," said Honeybody, who had the talent of being able to talk intelligibly while chewing, "I was thinking of taking it away from my Dodo, letting her think I was away on an undercover job."

Dodo, a raw-boned lady who operated a prosperous fish-and-chip emporium, was the Sergeant's helpmeet of thirty years.

"That's up to you."

"The thing is, they've got very good ale and nice old pubs, plus good coarse fishing in the river at Greymouth: and you've got a spare room. Besides, I'll contribute to the exes and two heads are better than one-about," the Sergeant chuckled richly, "1874 murders. Better find out what this millionaire wants, and give it to him. I can smell a nice fat bonus."

Harry managed to look shocked, feeling hypocritical as the thought had plainly occurred to him.

"My grandpa was on that case," said Honeybody, not too surprisingly as the family, then farm labourers, had leaped upon the bandwagon the day after Sir Robert Peel had started recruiting police.

"I think you once told me he was in the West Country."

Honeybody, whose memory as well as figure was elephantine, rubbed his square, protruding jaw. "He knew the woman, Penelope Fennel. Fine figure of a woman, robust with the accent on the second syllable. 'Course you could not see legs in those days unless they fell over. A big natural blonde. I remember old Grandpa chewing through his pipe stem one day when he was describing her. But guilty. He was a shrewd judge of character. You get to be that among these country villains."

The Sergeant disliked countryfolk of any description.

"Can you remember what he said?"

"He died when I was fourteen. But I eventually got his diaries. I've skipped through them. Dull routine stuff, but I've got them somewhere. The victim was an Army officer who was engaged to her. Motive, jealousy: *mod. op.*, antimony, the Victorian's friend in need. The victim's father brought down a lot of smart London legal talent which actually prejudiced the case in her favour. Besides, the family were very wealthy and a bit 'old' in the county sense. I'll try to find his diary."

Thus at seven a.m. one morning ten days later the Inspector, his wife Elizabeth, their rising three-year-old daughter Amanda, and the year-old twins, Cedric and William in order of seniority, embarked with Honeybody on the journey to Greymouth. The past few days had been a nightmare, for Elizabeth, who had recently joined the Conservative Party and learned about reverence for the head of the family, kept consulting him with huge lists of trivia. Should she take drip-dry or cotton? Harry did not care whether she took tarred paper. However the addition of Honeybody was quite acceptable to her. The Sergeant was good about the house, a handyman (which Harry was most definitely not), and children doted on him.

In his eagerness to get the task, the Inspector had thought it best not to broach the subject of expenses: a satisfactory job might result in the honorarium—yes, that was the name for it and, by God, it just might not be taxable—being suitably increased. So, motivated partly by the desire to keep his wife happy and partly by memories of train journeys with three children and a dog, he had hired a car from a company which gave reduced rates to policemen under the impression that they never drank.

Honeybody, Elizabeth and the children sat in the back. Harry drove, their enormous dog, Mr Bones, by his side. ("It'll be so much saving if we take him," his wife had said.)

Greymouth was not, as might be expected, a seaside resort or port. The name was one of those corruptions which so confuse the traveller in England. It was a town situated on the western mouth of a large and fertile valley, with broad farms and little industry except for the canneries which processed pork and vegetables, and more recently deep-freeze establishments which had started gobbling up the choicest crops. Greymouth achieved the rather sprawling sleepiness of West Country cathedral towns of a certain size: however bustling the street might be at certain times there was a soporific atmosphere overhead, almost a heaviness, perhaps due to the relaxing air. Greymouth Manor stood on a hill, a subtle house the attractions of which grew on you rather than forcing the eye at first acquaintance. But it was not to the house that Harry drove: instead the lodge-keeper on a bicycle guided them along a side path lined with a trim privet hedge.

They came to an old wall, and the lodge-keeper opened the gates. Driving for a hundred yards through a small orchard, culminating in a lawn with flower beds, they saw an L-shaped cottage. About a hundred years old, thought the Inspector. He stopped the car in the driveway, there apparently being no garage.

"Here's the key, sir," said the lodge-keeper. "Would you like me to show you round?"

Harry, rather wishing to minimise Mr Bones' presence because of what might well be a delicately furnished pad, said no.

"The name is Hodge, sir. There is a village lady who would come in for the Heavies three hours a day if wished." He had plainly totted up the children.

Harry prayed him to have the lady cope with the Heavies as from next morning and Elizabeth looked as though she was purring.

To their surprise the interior was surprisingly modern, and the furniture new, the two bathrooms reconditioned and the big kitchen something to arouse Elizabeth's envy. The beds were made, there was food in the fridge and a small but comprehensive array of bottles on the small bar. Only Honeybody was disconsolate. "They remembered gin, whisky and vodka, Harry, but clean forgot any beer or stout, though we might nip out later and load up."

The note on the kitchen table was short and to the point.

Dear Mr James,

I do hope you find everything comfortable: telephone my housekeeper if not.

Perhaps you might like to drop round tonight at six for a drink. Pray bring Mrs James if she can leave the children.

Yours sincerely,
CHARLES FENNEL.

"I can't go anyway," snarled Elizabeth over his shoulder, "you never told me to bring a cocktail dress."

"Go as you are, ducks," said Honeybody.

"You are both impossible." She flounced off to the kitchen.

Spread out in one of the three reception rooms were neatly labelled files, a portable typewriter and accessories, and a tape-recorder.

Over the past ten days, the Inspector, partly from the feeling that he was going to be paid for doing it, partly because of the work load, had refrained from looking up the Fennel Case, as it was known, although the victim was a Captain Bradstreet, of the Thirteenth Fencible Foot, stationed at the military barracks on the outskirts of the town.

Honeybody, capable of sustained work when pushed, had typed out four foolscap pages from his grandfather's diary.

"Have a look at some of this stuff," said Harry. "There is a summary for me to read."

Penelope Joan deWitt Fennel had celebrated her twenty-sixth birthday on June the seventeenth, 1874. It was a grand day at Greymouth Manor, the Great Ballroom, at a cost of one thousand pounds, having been transformed into a tropical garden, complete with waterfalls, pineapple bushes and stuffed birds, for the occasion was the announcement of her betrothal to Captain Bradstreet. It was considered a good match. The prospective bridegroom was the only son of Sir Ferguson Bradstreet, the thirteenth Baronet. He was not present at the ball and sent no excuse. By the legal fiction current he and his son had broken the entail on their land when John was twenty-one.

(The Inspector remembered you got the prospective purchaser to sue you for wrongful possession and did not contest.)

Father and son received twenty thousand pounds each. Sir Ferguson had had a career at Court and in return for whatever services he had rendered had a pension of two thousand a year. For some years he had lived in dissolute retirement in apartments off the Strand and was reputed to have nothing left but his pension, a malicious disposition, and a choleric temper. There was a small sheaf of photographs in colour (Sir Charles had been that thorough) of prints and paintings. The Inspector stared for a few long seconds at Sir Ferguson in Court Dress—Comptroller of the Spice Room as he had been. The face was long and red, the eyes so small and close set as to look like currants set in a painted vegetable marrow.

It was a fortunate match for the gallant Captain. Penelope Fennel was the only sister of James Fennel (Sir Charles' grandsire) the apple of whose eye she was. The rapport between them was very strong, said the summary. Though an heiress (she had seventy thousand pounds for which James was her Trustee) she chose not to maintain a separate establishment. Instead James had built for her a house called the Cottage in the grounds of the Manor. There she lived with a female companion, one Mrs Gunter, a poor widow, and a lady's maid. Other domestic help, four in number, came in during the day. Her carriage and horses were kept in the main stabling.

She had been educated by governesses as was usual at the time, except for two years at an exclusive academy in France from the age of seventeen. She was considered rather better read than most young ladies, which may have accounted for the fact that though her fair, Brunhilde looks were so much to the prevailing male taste, and indeed she was one of the most toasted debutantes, she seemed not to have had a serious "offer" until she met the Captain, when one of a party who visited the regimental ball. The Captain's wooing was swift, possibly abetted by James Fennel, who wished to see his sister "settled", and his wife (though not, it was to transpire, from the same motives). Within a month the engagement was announced and the wedding settled for September the fourth, the happy pair to honeymoon in Italy for a month before returning to the Cottage, which was James Fennel's wedding present.

The Captain had explained that since he was on such bad terms with his father there could be no wedding settlement from that quarter. Perhaps blinded by his sister's happiness, perhaps a little overawed by the social position of the Bradstreets—though wealthy landowners and squires the Fennels were nevertheless "in trade" and of no great origin—James Fennel seemed to have taken it for granted that there was substantial entailed property which in the course of time would pass with the title into the Captain's hands.

In fact at the time of his engagement the Captain was in the hands of money-lenders to whom he owed three thousand pounds. He was being pressed, with the dire possibility of bankruptcy and the loss of his commission. He seems, said the précis, to have been a calculating man, yet handsome and popular and without the malice that characterised his father. His financial downfall was due to his fondness for associating with those whose fortunes were not twenty thousand pounds, but twenty thousand per year, and who thought little of a two-hundred-pound wager. The Captain was not a particularly enthusiastic gambler, but in his "set" an occasional flutter was "the thing" and he was dead unlucky.

In 1874 the Captain was thirty-four and since the age of twenty-six had kept a mistress in a small villa at Herne Hill, London. She was a pretty, penniless daughter of a failed stationer, educated "above her class", and the Captain was madly in love. They had two children, aged two and seven.

Upon his engagement he did not break off the association. The mistress was not called at the Inquest—apparently by the specific request of Penelope Fennel.

"I wonder why?" said Harry James to the Sergeant.

"Double-edged weapon. It would have got her sympathy in one way, but maybe strengthened motive in another. Besides the mistress might have known something."

The first trouble started when the question of Penelope's money came up. In those days before the Married Women's Property Act, the husband had complete control of all assets. James Fennel, now head of the family business and the apotheosis of the Victorian male, rather approved. Not so his sister. She had no objection to allowing her husband to have entire control of the income, but stubbornly insisted that the principal should be settled upon her. Bradstreet made some fuss about this. There were tiffs and sweet reconciliations. A climax came when Penelope blandly said that of course the Cottage and its contents would be included in the Settlement.

"To sit on every chair on sufferance, as if under a landlady's roof. Good God," said the Captain, "you insult my honour, ma'am. What has come into you, Penny?" he added less theatrically. Witness to this scene, which occurred in the sitting-room of the Cottage, was the companion, Mrs. Gunter, a half-French lady of mannish aspect who was more and more to come into the story.

"Of course," said Harry to Honeybody, "he wanted cash to settle his debts. He had apparently borrowed another two thousand at 'reasonable' interest—a mere twenty per cent. Gosh, those were the days! Security was his 'prospects'. As far as concerns what had come into her, I guess she was a chip off the old block of Scottish ironfounders, perhaps not quite so blinded as the Captain might have imagined."

In the end the lady weakened, and the property was kept out of the Settlement. While Penelope lived high on the hog, her brother as trustee allowed her freely to handle her income. In the Season she moved into the Town House in Belgrave Square with her brother and sister-in-law, Annie. Her hunters were part of the string kept by James, for show rather than utility as far as he himself was concerned, she had free access to James' great wine cellar—he was something of a *bon viveur*—and the produce of the home farm, kitchen gardens and hot-houses was hers to command. Her one extravagance was dress, so over the years she had accumulated the sum of seventeen thousand pounds on deposit with Messrs Coutts.

Bradstreet, who appeared through the mists of time to have had a glib tongue, had told her at the end of July some story of being let down in a business deal, and having to have five thousand to tide him over until matters were settled up. He appeared reluctant to take the money, but she pressed it on him. With this he apparently commissioned a friend—one of those "men of business" who specialised in getting young swells out of their financial folly for a price—to buy in his bills on the money-lending market. In those days it was common for a money-lender to give in cash less than the face value of the bill. For a bill for one hundred one might get sixty pounds in cash "plus other valuable considerations". The bill itself might change hands for more or, often, considerably less. So was footnoted the précis.

Shortly before this transaction, Bradstreet, who was in London for the week-end, announced that "everything was off".

At the Inquest much was made of this. It was suggested that it was part of the motive. Penelope and her family denied any knowledge of it. Her senior counsel, Sir Robert Chaffanbrass, suggested that it was a rumour started by deceased with the object of depreciating the value of his own paper. One Mr McPherson who dealt in such matters deposed that he had sold one thousand pounds' worth at face value, for two hundred pounds, upon hearing the rumour. "No good 'anging on in this game."

As the accepted suitor, Captain Bradstreet was often at the Cottage. Harry realised that the Victorians were rather deceptive as far as prudishness was concerned, though of course the resident maid and Mrs Gunter were theoretically around, but, as the remorseless cross-examination at the Inquest (Sir Edmund Socket, instructed by Mr Brewer, and fee'd by Sir Ferguson Bradstreet) established, very often they were not.

At week-ends the Captain was the guest of James and Annie Fennel at the Manor, an establishment conducted with considerable magnificence. As the Captain sampled his host's quite famous wine cellar, ate the dishes prepared by two French chefs and a pastry-cook, strolled in the magnificent gardens, he must have thought that all a man might desire was within his reach. It had been agreed that he would continue his Army career, perhaps obtaining a Colonelcy in another "fencible" regiment, one which never served abroad.

Except perhaps love. There were two week-ends at Herne Hill with his *de facto* wife and children.

Bradstreet's motivation was an obscure business, thought Harry. Did he subconsciously desire to "break the connexion" as the Victorians had it? Against his future brother-in-law's advice, he handled Penelope most undiplomatically, criticising her extravagance—of all persons to do so—and among other things threatening to dismiss the companion, Mrs Gunter, upon returning from their Italian honeymoon. Mrs Gunter herself always denied that she knew this, but Penelope said that several quarrels had taken place at the Cottage upon the subject. Both the Captain and Penelope, when roused, had Bashan-like voices, and Miss Penelope's vocabulary was "not befitting a gentlewoman" (see evidence by the Vicar, the Rev Horace Trotwin, who, however, was on bad terms with the Unitarian Fennel family). The author of a paper on the subject, published in 1928, suggested that each got sexual satisfaction from this bellowing, marital brawling often having "a sexual/emotional context".

The Fatal Evening. On August the seventeenth, a Friday, the Captain had appeared to his fellow officers distraught and not his usual genial extrovert self. He was popular with the men, in a rough, bullying manner, because he understood them and rarely put them on a charge, preferring the abrasive edge of his tongue. That day he "crimed" six privates. At four thirty, his duty at an end, he changed into civilian clothes and rode over to the Cottage. He and his fiancée had been invited to dine at eight at the Manor, but had declined a couple of days before. As it was the arrangement stood that he would have something with Penelope and Mrs Gunter, spend an hour or so in the drawing-room—neither lady objected to cigars—and depart for his quarters in the barracks at around ten. The road, although in those days running between hedgerows heavy with dog-roses and wildflowers, was excellently surfaced with Tarmacadam and the night, although not moonlit, was far from dark.

Evidence was to the effect that Bradstreet had drunk fairly heavily. More than heavily according to modern standards, thought Harry, but in those days not more than "giving the demon a bit of a nudge". It was his habit, a common one among horsemen in those days, to carry a curved hip flask of silver and pigskin, a small cup fitting over the plug. In his case, he carried brandy and during the meal he produced the flask, telling Penelope that he would be grateful if she would have it filled.

"I'll see to it myself, Captain," she said formally, and briefly rising placed it on one of those useless little sub-shelves sported by sideboards of the day.

The hangman passed very close to Miss Fennel at that moment.

However, assuming that the Captain had finished all or part of the flask, which held six fluid ounces of brandy when filled, he already had a solid basis upon which to consume a half a bottle of hock, two bottles of burgundy and three kümmels which he did while eating consommé, whiting with a cheese sauce, roast beef and trimmings, a sorbet and Stilton cheese. Both ladies had hearty appetites, but that night neither drank much. (On occasion Miss Fennel was inclined to be over-fond of liqueurs: evidence of her sister-in-law.)

During the meal a quarrel developed. The Captain's ruddy face gradually turned darker and his remarks became more personal. He made devious comments about the iniquity of prying, of women trying to be men (a homosexual relationship between the two women had been speculated upon by commentators but there seemed to be no evidence at all; the particular remark was heard by the two maids who waited at table) and of wanton extravagance. The embarrassed Mrs Gunter made some excuse to retire to the drawing-room where she got out her embroidery but for some reason felt too upset to take up her needle. It was twenty minutes before she heard the bell ring for the maids to clear away and almost immediately the Captain and Miss Penelope joined the companion.

(Nothing further was said about the flask : Penelope maintained she had opened the sideboard, taken out a decanter of brandy kept there, along with sherry, Bual, and assorted liqueurs, and given it and the flask to the Captain, who filled it. She said his hand shook and one of the maids deposed that burgundy and brandy had been liberally spilt on the cloth.)

In the drawing-room the atmosphere was constrained and the talk less than small. At nine thirty the Captain said he had a full day on the morrow (a lie) and must be going. Penelope showed him to the front door and went out into the night with him. The Inspector looked out of the window. The orchard had not been planned then, the neat plan showed an old English garden. It had been a lightish night, one of those when the sky becomes luminous and the smell of summer perfume hangs upon heavy air.

Penelope said they talked for a quarter of an hour. The Captain was contrite and promised to sever his connexion with "that woman".

(It seemed Penelope never knew that the two children were the Captain's.)

At the time of the engagement, Penelope had caused temporary stabling to be constructed for the Captain's horse, not much more than a shed. When he was expected one of the grooms came over from the Manor, remaining with the horse until the Captain required it. That day, it was a big mare of sixteen hands, but "quiet as an old dove" (*vide* the groom). He had groomed and fed her, replacing saddle and bridle half an hour previously. The Captain, in the light of an oil lamp, looked tired and very flushed, but he perfunctorily thanked the man and tossed him half a crown. Then he trotted off into the night and that was the last anybody saw of him alive.

At one in the morning the mare went into her stabling at the barracks, where the soldier on night duty proved a regular Soldier Schweik, driving Sir Robert Chaffanbrass, for Miss Penelope, and Sir Edmund Socket, for Sir Ferguson Bradstreet, into a state of tearing hair from their wigs, or wigs from their hair, realised Harry. A superb example of know-nothing, he apparently saw little untoward in riderless mares entering his establishment in the early hours ("Stands to reason," he had beamed from the witness stand, " 'osses carnt 'ave people on 'em all the bloomin' time"). At any rate in the morning Bradstreet's fellow officers, discovering that his room was unoccupied, "covered up" for him, and it was not until noon that it was noticed that both his horses were in their stalls. The Colonel was an efficient man and sent out a mounted patrol, at the same time dispatching a messenger at the gallop to the Cottage. Miss Fennel had taken her carriage to lunch with a friend (twisted into callousness of conduct in the deranged nightmare of the Inquest) but Mrs Gunter provided the necessary information.

But it was not until four that six small children, seeking daisies, saw the Captain, one arm spasmodically jerking, lying in a deep ditch inside a hedgerow, through which in his agony he must have crawled. There was a trail of vomit, but nobody thought to take a sample. It was an hour later before the eldest child summoned courage enough to tell "our mum" and near enough eight before he was bedded in the officers' sick bay at the barracks.

It would be easy enough to blame the Regimental Surgeon, but he was not seasoned or trained in poisoning. He gave the Captain a massive dose of laudanum which knocked him out, and diagnosed internal injuries caused by falling off a horse. The Colonel telegraphed Sir Ferguson Bradstreet and sent a messenger to James Fennel, who, without disturbing his sister who had been in her room with a migraine headache since returning from lunch, took a fast pony and a trap over immediately. He was a shrewd man and not liking what he saw immediately telegraphed to Sir Howard Dill, greatest physician of his generation, to take a special train at the first available occasion, with necessary nurses and equipment for suspected internal injuries.

All in all, worked out Harry, this would have cost James close on five hundred pounds, for the special train at a pound per mile, Sir James at the same, plus incidentals. A good sum, even if a beloved sister's happiness was involved. James must have smelled a rat, said Harry's instinct.

Sir Howard arrived at one o'clock. In fact the train service was faster in 1874 than in 1969 when they closed the Greymouth loop line and all stations attached to it.

At one thirty he was saying: "There are no internal injuries, this is poison."

In his sleep the wretched Captain had been sick again, enabling Sir Howard to collect a small specimen which had remained unnoticed on the bed-clothes. In the morning it was placed on the mail train addressed to the pathologist at Guy's Hospital.

There was little more to do until Bradstreet recovered consciousness, but Sir Howard was already settled in his mind that a massive dose of either antimony or, more remotely, arsenic had been taken. The physician had his bed made up in an ante-room and slept while the two nurses watched Bradstreet, who recovered consciousness at six in the morning and was quite rational, to the extent that would have deceived many doctors.

"I remember getting off the mare before the pain got

bad," he presently told Sir Howard. "After that I dimly remember crawling."

"Captain, you have taken something!"

The dying man shook his head violently and the doctor pressed him no further.

That day Penelope arrived shortly after ten o'clock. Again Bradstreet, washed and combed by the ubiquitous nurses, had staged the partial recovery so typical of antimonial poisoning.

He accepted Penelope's kiss and talked of their approaching wedding, but after ten minutes the nurses signalled for her to leave. At noon the Captain's condition had worsened. Sir Howard wasted no words: "Captain Bradstreet, you are dying. There is no hope. For the sake of the living, tell us what you took."

Huskily, his voice bubbling between cracked lips, Bradstreet replied: "I took nothing that would kill me."

Later in the afternoon, he rallied again, and the Regimental Chaplain prayed with him, after which he dictated a short five-line Will, leaving anything he possessed to his mistress. By that time Guy's Hospital had telegraphed a preliminary finding of "massive" antimony. The Captain seemed calm and collected and a nurse spoke of his sweet smile. Shortly before six Penelope saw him again. The two nurses testified that she, in tears, knelt at the bedside. Bradstreet said, laboriously, "Pen... Penny... it was so wrong..." Then he fell back unconscious. Sir Howard strove officiously with heart injections, but Bradstreet did not speak again until he went out with the tide at three a.m. next morning.

Now neither the Regiment nor the vested interests wanted scandal. Officers did not take poison—what an example to the men! Neither were they poisoned—what a temptation to the men! The Fennel Estate encompassed nearly every shopkeeper and small farmer in the district, plus most of the licensed houses (they owned the small brewery) and nobody wished an upheaval. An unhappy landlord can be a vicious landlord, so prompted racial memory. With all this went the Deputy Coroner for the district, a fat old man named Tomkin who had been jobbed through his solicitor's articles when the post, a very minor plum, fell into the hands of the Tomkin family. The problem of providing for huge Victorian families was more or less solved by the condition of the drains and the ignorance of medical science, but perversely every Tomkin child clung to life, so that the minor branches of the family were an importunate sponge upon the Viscount Tomkin, who obstinately held on to Government office for the purposes of being employment officer for the clan. The best his father, occupying the same position, had been able to do was to provide the reversion of a deputy coronership for the then young Tomkin.

The fly in the ointment was Sir Ferguson Bradstreet. Captain Bradstreet was the last of the line, no other heirs existing. It might have been partly pride of lineage that actuated Sir Ferguson. However he had always hated Penelope, and for no reason. Bradstreet had taken her to the old man's apartment for a formal presentation and he was barely civil, thereafter referring to her as "the blacksmith's daughter", an allusion to the Fennel iron interests.

Upon hearing of his son's death, and its nature, old Bradstreet hurried round to Mr James Gerald, solicitor, at his comfortable premises in Jermyn Street. Shortly before those days there had been no respectable solicitors specialising in criminal law and divorce. This was the recognised province of pettifoggers and ambulance chasers with whom counsel dealt via their clerks. Mr Gerald changed all that, with his dignified premises, his two academic paintings ("Augustus rendering Justice" and "The Trial of Charles I") his discreet, superbly dressed clerks. His oily manner and outwardly gentlemanly aspect gained him a goldmine the existence of which his colleagues had never suspected. He listened impassively to the quiet torrent of venom which poured from the old gentleman, reflecting in his pre-Freudian way that there must have been a lot of *sub rosa* screwing around the Court and that old Bradstreet obviously felt he hadn't had his fair share.

"We must brief Sir Edmund Socket for the Inquest," he said, as his thoughts ran encyclopaedically over credit rating. The old man could probably raise three thousand at a pinch. "That will be two hundred and fifty guineas and fifty per day refresher, but well worth it as he is the most deadly cross-examiner today. We must retain him at once before your, before the Fennels get him."

The Fennels' solicitor, a shrewd old countryman, did not in fact suggest Socket, but rather Sir Robert Chaffanbrass, veteran, household word, expert at what cricketers call "a dead bat". He charged four hundred guineas on acceptance plus eighty guineas per day "refresher", it all dating from the days before the standard coin was reduced from twenty-one shillings to twenty, a fact conveniently ignored by the Bar.

The Press, tipped off by the clerk employed by Mr Gerald, the originator of public relations, showed their shark-like teeth and the Government decided that "Mr Attorney" should attend on behalf of the Crown, this being, remembered the Inspector, almost exactly two years before the Crown was extended to fit India as well.

Harry pushed away the empty plate of sandwiches which Elizabeth had brought in.

"How goes it?"

"She did it," said Honeybody, "no doubt about it." His great hands held the extract from his grandfather's diary.

August 17, 1874. Very hot and stifling and Barbie has the cold she always gets in summer. Pigs sick, Dick having fed 'em cold bacon. Thrashed him. Great honour that the Chief wishes me to go with him to Miss Penelope. There are rumours at the ale house that the Captain was poison'd. He was an open handed man much liked and thrashed Tim Baines with his whip when he caught Tim thrashing his wife, tho' not much good as he black'd her eye and kicked her shamefully when the Captain had gone.

Later. Miss Penelope v. nervous, cannot understand why. The Chief said, Miss Penelope, the poor Captain succoured (*sic*) to poison. She said was it laudanum, he suffered from his gums and used to rub it on.

Nothing much more but was shocked: have seen women quite like it before when trying to conceal Births etcetera.

The Chief asked me did I know the servants. I said yes and he says to make Discreet Inquiries with Liberal Exes.

The Honeybodys had not changed so much over the two generations, thought Harry amused. He felt no great emotion. Generally murder made him either indignant to the point of dull rage or just fed up. This produced a certain weary, embalmed cynicism.

"The Inquest lasted four days," he said, "and was nasty. They even questioned the poor lady about Certain Familiarities she had allowed the Captain after a good dinner."

"Pinching her bot., eh?" Honeybody disengaged his belly

from the table's edge. "Gawd knows how they did it with all those skirts."

"They had little trap doors with buttons set in the back," said the Inspector primly.

"But the corsets. But the corsets," said the Sergeant. "Break a thumb-nail on 'em as quick as nothing. I remember seeing 'em flapping on the clothes-lines as a boy."

"Love will find a way. Lord I must run."

"I'll have a look at the town," said Honeybody, "and lay in anything Elizabeth might want."

11

GIVEN A SOUND structure age can beautify. The Manor had been a sensibly designed house fit for a man who intended to have thirteen children, God knew how many dependants, servitors, hanger-on, visitors, old pensioners and visiting dignitaries under his roof. Time had mellowed it, working it as it were into the landscape which, thanks to the fortune made out of World War One and subsequently town planning, had escaped practically unscathed apart from a line of pylons which the eye got used to.

Most of the land was let to a deep-frozen food company. The home farm was a small private corporation. Two-thirds of the rooms of the Manor had been treated with chemicals and firmly closed, but the remainder was magnificent and sported a veritable butler, a young man with longish hair, who escorted the Inspector into a kind of sub drawing-room, of the lavish kind which always set the Inspector back because it could never be conducive to slippered unbuttoned ease, feet on the fender, quart of ale on the floor beside the club chair, well-worn favourite books on one wall, which symbolised his philosophy. He had to admit it was elegant, a bit out of a Beaton set for a Wilde play.

Sir Charles Fennel was a tall man with what the Victorians described as a "high colour". The hair, once no doubt of the peculiar straw colour found only among those of Scottish ancestry, had achieved a neutral colour between white and yellow. It had thinned so that the ivory scalp showed underneath like the base of a frayed carpet. He had frosty blue eyes and a craggy face. He greeted the Inspector warmly and introduced his wife.

It came as something of a shock to realise that she was American. God knows why, but one hardly expected to find a fortyish—to be kind—elegant little blonde from (judging by her accent) Illinois seated, or rather insouciantly perched, on the gilt Regency chair straight out of Brighton Pavilion. The Inspector explained that his wife was tied by three young children: Lady Fennel said she could recommend a reliable sitter and should they have provided cots. Harry mentioned that they had brought portable ones for the twins. (His eldest, Amanda, had insisted on a double bed: he hoped the girl would turn out all right.)

Harry immediately mentioned Honeybody, and the frosty eyes dropped in temperature ten degrees. Sir Charles was not a man who liked to be unconsulted.

"I went through a lot of red-tape to get him," said Harry. "His grandfather accompanied the Chief Constable to see Miss Penelope and kept a diary."

"From a local family!" Sir Charles thawed umpteen degrees. Had he been a bullock on the home farm Harry was sure he would have been patted.

"Indeed, Sir Charles, indeed."

The martinis were perfect as were the savouries.

"What is your first impression?" at length asked his host. "The consensus was that she was guilty, as you well know."

"I've always been unhappy about it." said Lady Fennel, and the Inspector, with some unease, recognised the do-good tones underlying the Bryn Mawr and Chicago accent. "And of course it is a stain on the scutcheon sort of thing, so we thought to rehabilitate her in a book."

No harm in that, thought Harry, several of whose friends were literary men who borrowed small sums and generally repaid them. The Victorian age, when forensic medicine, thanks to Professor Taylor, was creeping warily from its shell, redounded with equivocal murder trials. One year Poodle would write a "she was guilty" book: next year Quoodle was commissioned to prove innocence: the well-known Oxford Don came in later with a balanced survey which pointed to no murder at all. Finally the well-known writer advanced the theory that the only person who could not have done it actually had. No harm in it at all, but he wished the photographs were not so dull.

"You are sceptical," teased her ladyship. "Tell me, Inspector, you think we are feeing you to bolster a brief our way, huh?"

"The thought occurred to me," said Harry, realising that he was eating stuffed field mushrooms instead of cultivated.

"I'll tell it," said Sir Charles and for the next few minutes was thoroughly thawed before retreating into deep freeze. "You have observed that the Cottage has recently been modernised? An old friend, not well Endowed with Worldly Goods (Sir Charles slyly dismissed it like halitosis or a social disease contracted by Youthful Folly) needs a year's sabbatical, so we have a little plot to install him and his wife there. Since my great-aunt's death—and I think that she deliberately killed herself by taking mad risks in the hunting field—it has been only intermittently occupied by senior Estate employees. Now there is a different set-up and for five years it was empty. I decided to modernise. Everything was 1870 or earlier so I got a dealer down who gave me a lump sum, a remarkably large one it seemed to me. But what he did not want was the wardrobe in what had been Penelope's bedroom. It was immense, m' dear fellow, immense, a tomb in itself to hold a royal family plus some politicians. You know the sort of thing?"

The Inspector did.

"It must have been built inside the bedroom. It was too big to bring out through the window or the doors and it had not been assembled from sections. I thought, frankly, of sending a man in with an axe to break it up into kindling for the occasional log fire. However, my wife happened to look at it and, presto, spotted it was a rare and beautiful Australian wood. There was a vogue in the seventies to support the colonies by buying their fancy timber. I must say that when you peered at it it was superb. It so happens that we are building—to his own design, and, m' dear fellow, bloody awful it will look but there we are—a house for our son on the outskirts of town, and m' wife had the idea of using this wonderful wood in it. So we got old, or rather young (the old man having had his fourth stroke) Cryer who does our carpentry to take a look. He almost cried. Stroked it as if it were..." Sir Charles cleared his throat and left it at that. "Anyway young Cryer took it reverently to pieces. Apparently the thing was infested with what I shall call 'semi-secret' drawers. No Sexton Blake secret-spring kind of things, but little hidey-holes the maids would not know about..."

"And he discovered this," said Lady Fennel, whipping a thin book from underneath her chair. It was covered by the repugnant, green scaly leather so popular in the seventies and eighties. "It was her diary, commenced in January 1873 culminating in December 1874. From her engagement in June until the end of the Inquest in November it is the diary of Agony and Ecstasy."

Oh God, thought Harry, but after all Americans were all novelists manqué. He wondered whether she was Jewish, they seemed to write all the American novels these days.

"He'd put her in the family way, Inspector," said Sir

Charles matter-of-factly, "and she had a miscarriage three days after his death."

Jumping off the kitchen table, no doubt, thought Harry gloomily.

"Tell me," demanded Lady Fennel, "what putative mother would murder the father of her unborn child—against all instinct, all logic?"

His wife, thought the Inspector, well not actual physical harm but with a bit of smart nagging—get up and feather the nest for the newcomer sort of thing or get your fat arse out of that chair and start painting the spare room.

Weakly, he nodded.

He threw a pebble. "Why should she conceal the diary?"

"It would have signed her death warrant," said Lady Fennel. "In those days they judged you partly on your sexual morals, or rather they judged women so. All the jury, a row of hypocritical men, would think of was the danger to their own spotty-faced daughters if fornication was allowed to go on the rampage among the lower middle classes. My, times change."

She had something there, realised Harry. Under the Victorian morality the lady always took the can back except the smarter society ones who became blackmailers. "Can I have it?" he asked.

"Take the holograph," said Sir Charles. "It has been micro-filmed. I thought I'd get Richard McSweet to do the book. One thousand guineas and a villa in Capri for three months, plus expenses, to do the actual finish."

"I keep telling Sir Charles that McSweet has whitewashed everybody from James I—paid by the Presbytery—to Goering, paid by some industrialists. And those great, purple organ notes."

"Perhaps one of the more severe lady novelists," suggested

Harry. "I mean in a book of this sort it is the reviews which are read, and they don't take much notice of McSweet since he made that terrible mistake about the King's Evil in his *Panoply of the Thirties*. A good lunch for the critics to launch it, sir, but with the finest wine and plenty of it, and tell the staff to turn a blind eye if they carry bottles away. Very plain food, because they all have nervous dyspepsia and short sight. To see them eating anything runny is rather distressing."

"You might be right," said Sir Charles, very much Chairman, "I leave it to you, Agnes, only do not make the final payment until you have the manuscript... you remember the trouble we had with the house-painters last year. My wife," he said rather shyly, "is rather the recondite literary end of the partnership."

They beamed at each other.

The Inspector spent five minutes dipping into the book. Hyperbole and blurb aside, it was the diary of a woman in love, bruised by each unkind word, scabbing over the cut by harsh words in her turn. And yet...

"I have to speak as a policeman," said Harry, "and diaries and suchlike records are faked every day. Every absconding accountant has his office festooned with them. This might have been her Last Alibi. If tried, she might have made herself the devoted lover, the Captain the licentious cad. You say, Lady Fennel, that the Victorian juries convicted on sexual prejudice, but surely only on adultery. Seduction of a maiden by the male was never considered a motive. I refer you to Madeline Smith... who emigrated to the United States, by the way." (The remark was not particularly appreciated by his hostess.)

"He's right, you know," said Sir Charles, clearly a factual fiend, "her husband was quite well known in the wall-paper manufacturing business. She went to the States when he died."

"I must say," said Harry, "that if this diary, or excerpts from it, and taking into account today's thinking, is genuine it should exonerate her completely."

"Then she can rest in peace," said Lady Fennel, looking at the clock.

"No, don't go," said her husband, "we are not dining until eight. Would have asked you, but we have quite a delegation of house guests. German businessmen, God bless them. You can always try to stuff them at lunchtime, but they never sleep, always tugging their eighteen stones around with awkward questions. Much prefer Spanish who you never see after eleven in the morning."

"Or before ten," said Lady Fennel with a giggle. "One never knows whether it is sleep or sex with them."

"From the detective point of view it is both, larded by a lot of gossip," said Harry.

"I do want an unbiased opinion about the case," said Sir Charles.

"He certainly took antimony," said Harry, "that is one point beyond all issue. The stuff is colourless and does not taste, unless you are *looking* for a taste. If you need a glass of wine or spirits to give you a kick then you drain it. With antimony it takes about five minutes before you start the first cramps. It absorbs into the system fast. The Victorians were always mucking about with the stuff. In very small doses it was reputed to cure compulsive drinking. You fed it to hubbie and every time he took a tot he vomited, in theory building up a repugnance to hard drink. Then they gave it to horses—arsenic as well—to perk them up and shine their coats, only from the evidence your grandpapa would not have the stuff on the property."

"The Victorians," said Sir Charles, "treated dangerous drugs like kids treat fireworks. Even so you could not get antimony without being known by the chemist. None was ever traced here, my grandfather having this horror of drugs and poisons—and he lived to be eighty-three."

"There seemed to be no sustained effort to pinpoint the supply of poison," said Harry, "though half the stables around had a small jar of it in the groom's tackle-room. However, unless your ancestress—is that the word?—was a Borgia, the diary proves her innocence. Why not just have that published?"

"We would wish," said Lady Fennel, "to suggest the rightful culprit. There was Mrs Gunter, you know, and the Mistress."

"I once read an article stating it was the lady's maid who suffered from unrequited love," said Harry grimly. "A lady novelist put that one up."

"Well," said Sir Charles, with the unconscious habit of a Chairman brightly dismissing his managers with insoluble problems, "that's that. Do you ride, Mr James?"

The Grey Goat, the nearest pub to the Cottage, was opposite an old church. Both were run down and had seen better days, and shared an egalitarian quality. In the church the old curtained private pews had been demolished and the landlord of the pub had torn down the dividing partitions so that it was in fact all one long bar, an experiment which had proved popular while still preserving the old grouping. Old Symes, doyen of the farm labourers, still occupied part of the space traditionally fenced off for him and his fellows, though the younger breed, gentry and peasants, tended to look alike and intermingle. Unerringly the Sergeant loomed upon a little group around old Symes, leered envelopingly, and ordered a light and bitter.

"I've seen that face before," said Symes, aged ninety-five and still employed in a carping capacity by the long-suffering Vicar who farmed eight acres at a loss.

"Name of Honeybody."

"The old Sergeant's son," said Symes without emotion. "Many a time he's kicked my arse. Fine big, lusty man he wore. You won't ever be his strapper."

"Grandson," said Honeybody.

"That's it, that's it," howled Symes, "the blood's runnin' thin. Got children?"

"Six," said Honeybody and the old fellow looked disappointed.

"In the polis?"

"Sergeant."

"Got no education," explained the illiterate Mr Symes. "Anybody with five O levels gets to be an Inspector these days, without a brain in their little old 'eads. Down about the buggery as usual, eh? Why they trouble about it year after year, sendin' down the Red Judge, fairly mazes me."

"Penelope Fennel," said the Sergeant, and the company looked mystified, except for old Symes. "She done it," he said soberly, "a rare jealous family ... as they was then," he hastened to add with a sideways glance. "A big, lusty wench ... I never actually saw her that I can remember but the bigger boys 'ad stories of the way she'd look ... ar, but she got a comeuppance when Pride of May, as devilish an 'orse as you ever see, threw her on the rocks in Teachers' Brook. They say her 'ead was a rare sight, a rare sight." Abruptly the old man lost interest.

"Better not get him off about the Fennels," murmured a spotty-faced man, who by his bulbous nose was perhaps a great-grandson, "because Ralf Fennel, the bald bloke behind the double Chivas Royal, is touchy about the family honour." He snickered.

"Ta ta for now," said the Sergeant. Old Symes was denouncing football pools, which he had got mixed up with roulette and Edward VII.

A bore, a sad, beastly bore, decided the Sergeant as he walked catlike beneath the high windows. All things to many people, the Sergeant felt all the contempt of a man who could switch "life and soul of the party" on, even if he felt rather ill, for the perennial, out-going bore, the pathetic man hanging on to the coat-tails of the crowd, so earnest and so anecdotal given the drop of the hat. Ralf Fennel sat alone with the smug expression common to bores. Was there nervousness and frustration beneath? The Sergeant, although a good judge of coarse human fishing, was never sure.

"Excuse the liberty, sir, I'm sure," he breathed. "Name of Honeybody, Sergeant in the police."

"My car?" It was once "my wife" or "the children" thought Honeybody gloomily. Now it was their effing chariots.

"The Yard, sir, Sir Charles..."

"Oh, yes, that damned business! A whim of his wife, as if she's not on every do-gooding committee in six counties. Still, a very fine woman, y'know. I thought he'd got a Chief Inspector down."

"His humble assistant," said Honeybody, "and useful for the fact that the granfer was Sergeant here when the sad occurrence took place in 1874."

For a minute Ralf was very still, massaging his heavy

black jowls, a small pear-shaped man who was not unimpressive.

"I don't see the point in raking over old coals, Sergeant, and I think she did it . . . though Sir Charles and Lady Fennel are entitled to their illusions. Do you know about the diary?"

"News to me."

"It was found in an old wardrobe, *Ouida* stuff, gush and bosom-heaving. Sorry for herself. I always feel the ladies might spare a few tears for the men they torment. Get us tensed up and leave up at the front door, eh? Then run in and write their diaries. Huh. That's why I'm in a state of single blessedness. Huh."

Honeybody ordered another bottled ale, explaining carefully that he was forbidden to accept drinks while on any kind of duty, which was not true, but he was driving in strange country. He leaned forward, gave the car keys to the publican plus a massive order for beer and stout to be inserted into the boot and back seat. On second thoughts he added a Campari for Elizabeth, supposing there would be an expense account somewhere but in extremity prepared to donate it to that Junoesque lady.

"A diary would be a potent pointer to her innocence, sir," said the Sergeant.

"If true. Now what is a diary?"

"A record, sir."

"Precisely, and the first thing an absconding clerk, at the tea money, gravitating through stamps to customers' accounts, learns is to have a faked record. An excellent defence! When I was two I.C. in our little show in the desert . . ."

When you got drunk, the Sergeant reflected, was generally listening to fifty-year-old men telling you about their little show in the desert, from allusions to Madame Whatsername's cosy brothel in Casablanca which Jerry blew up with some Australian generals bedded down in it, to a salacious afterview of Cairo, that dull city, plus a great deal of military hindsight. He switched to tinned tomato juice which presumably came from Cornwall, judging by the mineral content: he would not have done so for himself, for Harry, or perhaps for Elizabeth, but he was godfather to one of the twins and some kind of inbred loyalty tweaked him even while he laughed at it.

"In Australia," the pear-shaped man eventually said, rousing the Sergeant from stupor, "we have in N.S.W. a Public Defender, who takes up these legal causes..."

Of course, the accent, registered Honeybody with a start, burly, a mite aggressive, sliding off into the nasal in moments of stress.

"Australian?"

Mr Fennel was amused and on another double Chivas Royal. "Oh I'm of a collateral cadet issue—sounds like a banker in forced labour, I must say. We come from the younger brother of the second Fennel, so to speak. The younger son took his gold and a clumsy old ship to Australia in 1822, and it was exactly thirty-one weeks before they made Sydney Heads. I have his diary and that was no kidding, brother. I do not think we could take it today, and having a bit of money he made it relatively soft, black pudding from the two pigs they kept on deck and bled once every four days."

"A hard school, sir."

"I wouldn't say that. Australians have been improvisors against a harsh environment. Here you were having poverty against plenty, Dickens and all that. Out there you likely had nothing against nothing. That's why Dickens never understood Australia."

"I'd better go," said the Sergeant.

"I run the local factory," said Ralf. "Phone me any time."

Elizabeth had made Swiss cheese fondue in the elegant container that ranked among the cookery equipment with the appropriate long-tined forks.

"Where did you get the Kirsch?" asked Harry.

"In the cupboard under the bar there is 'most anything. And you must speak sternly to Amanda about not grabbing down the ornaments."

Harry grunted and hoped there was something to follow. In spite of the canapés, he felt decidedly peckish and oddly relaxed. Murder cases customarily brought on his nervous dyspepsia, but balmed in antiquity as it was, the Fennel case was mental relaxation.

"What was she like?" enquired Elizabeth dipping.

"Who?"

"Lady Fennel, you fool. There's a very decent hock in the ice bucket if the Sergeant will cope."

"He is sixty-two-ish, she a well preserved Titian-haired forty-ish, Chicago at base, Bryn Mawr or similar at large, the scourge one gathers of the women's institutes, thinks Republican presidents are men of action, disapproves of free medicine but cries about native children. Has decided Penelope was done wrong by, there having been a diary discovered full of purple passages of lerve and self-abnegation."

"What was she wearing?"

"Wearing? You mean Lady Fennel? How the hell should I know? Underwear one fancies."

"You have the coarseness of the constabulary without its powers of observation."

"I think it might have been green."

"It's funny that a man never remembers what they have on," ruminated Moneybody, allowing himself a host's prerogative with the hock, "and if I may say so without offence a man can never quite remember what they look like in the buff, passion getting in the way of the visual nerves, a doctor once told me. It's a bit like Welsh rarebit with a drop of gin in it, like they put up at the better doss-houses. Fondue, eh?"

"You mustn't drop any bits of bread in the goo," said Elizabeth, "or it is drinks all round."

"Unhygienic," said Honeybody, spearing and slurping. "I mean if one of us has a fatal infection."

"You are both loathsome," said Elizabeth, "and from those disappointed eyes, I do have steak to follow with rather special 'taters."

"I met an old man who knew me grandad," said Honeybody, abandoning the fork and scooping with a slice of bread. "Always the same in the country, all your past sins and relatives recognised until doomsday. He said Penelope was a large, gamy bird with an eye on the men. Difficult in those days, a sneaky kiss in the conservatory and when do you want to see Father?"

"Long week-ends," said Harry, "was how they did it, with the dressing bell rung to get them sorted out into the right beds."

"I think that was for the marrieds," said Elizabeth. "I mean Victorian marrieds, of a certain class, used to sleep around but I do not think it much applied to the maidens. For heaven's sake, with grooms, butlers, ladies' maids and decayed chaperones what could a middle-class girl do? The workers did nothing but pray or drink or screw, taking their pick."

"It's amazing," said Honeybody, "what they have always been able to do. Love, me dear, will find a way, even in a disused 1942 air-raid shelter which I had in execution of my duty once to investigate. But for Miss Fennel, no!"

Elizabeth dished out the steak from the portable hot-plate. "I must say," she said, "that from a swift flip through the poor girl's diary, her heart was truly broken by this horse-riding, military, regulation-bashing brute."

Two pairs of hard professional eyes raked her. It was disconcerting, she thought, pouring sauce, how these nice shabby old tigers could suddenly turn man-eating.

"Was it a fake?" asked Harry. "She said in it that the Captain had seduced her and that in fact she was pregnant at his death. Not a thing to ingratiate her with a Victorian jury, but on the other hand at his decease he was going through with it. No Victorian male would dream you would knock off a bloke who was going to legitimise his issue."

"Such a horrible word, like publishing and promotions."

"Well, she'd have got off on the issue, the way she wrote it. Trouble is that I do not believe in diaries."

"Do you mean she faked it?"

"I think I'll have it loked at by an expert, for handwriting breaks in the first place, but more importantly whether she was faking it—writing a novel. A good literary man could probably tell where fiction began, words are used a bit different, so I understand. If so, she was a deadly lady."

"Motive, my dear?"

"Obsession, (*a*), to dominate: (*b*), to have sole possession of valuables she bought. At a guess I would say that the Captain manoeuvred her into a position where she was in a box, wedding coming up, amiably predatory bridegroom, brother (and in the final analysis keeper of her purse) dead set on the marriage."

"You are wrong, of course," said Elizabeth, awaiting praise for the distinctly unusual potatoes.

"My word, your cuisine gets better each nosh," said Honeybody, recognising the symptoms.

"It is the *pinchito* powder," said Elizabeth, aglow, "but you have to know exactly how much, just a touch to send the tongue into a little fire, or so the gentleman who sold it to me said."

"I must say it helps with the wind," said Honeybody. "Cumin and cayenne, isn't it?"

Elizabeth nodded doubtfully. "I think," she said, "you should take it at face value."

"I met another one of the Fennels down at the rubbidy," said Honeybody, "an old cock named Ralf Fennel. R A L F, so he was careful to tell me, an old family name."

"I rather got the impression that Charles was the last of the line, except for his son," said Harry.

"Remote cousins," said Honeybody. "Australia in the old days. Ralf coming over as an aftermath of the Second World War, and, if I take another hock, you will realise that I had a personally conducted tour through the desert. He was a gunner, or so I gathered when I flapped my ears open."

"I hope you did not insult him," said Harry, for the tenth time pushing Mr Bones' head from his lap. It was in practice impossible to remove the great hound from the underneath of a dining table, a position he occupied most days with the Inspector's daughter as company.

"I do not think you could do that," said Honeybody, watching the sizzling steaks on the hot-plate and presently spearing another.

"I cannot accept that she was guilty," said Elizabeth. "For what motive? For love? People do not kill for love, though in those days they sickened! For sex? My friends, that is easy for a woman to get, and don't look smug, Harry James."

"I have the impression, as I said before," said the Inspector, "that she felt herself boxed in. Very easy for Madame 1870 to feel, one imagines. I have—or had before the element of the diary entered into it—the impression that she was being nagged into marriage, oh, all sorts of subtle pressures, plus big ones from her brother whom she not only loved but respected, as Victorian women tended to do in the case of a dominant head of the family. Then she had the family acquisitiveness and saw the fortune she had inherited slipping from her hands into those of the Captain, and not being daft she must have known he had spendthrift fingers. He was a big, blond, whiskery, handsome, incipiently swag-bellied hunk of manhood, hail-well-met. I imagine she might really have liked a mousy little fellow like me." He leered at his wife. "Big dominating ladies do. The Captain was rather like Honeybody."

"I pinpointed why Mrs Gunter ratted," said Elizabeth. "On the fourth day of the Inquest that old devil—I can just imagine his sly eyes and his lisp..."

"You mean Sir Edmund Socket?" asked Harry, professionally on the side of the Establishment. "He went on to become Master of the Rolls, a most respected man and the only Armenian to hold high legal rank."

"He really bailed Mrs Gunter up," said Elizabeth. "You can almost see the poor little devil with two kids boarding at the Merchant Fishmongers' School, put there by James Fennel, who was an Alderman and a Governor of the School. Sir Edmund Socket kept on and on about one occasion when she left the drawing-room. She blushed and bridled and said she went to the ground-floor loo, just past the dining-room. She could have nipped in and poisoned the flask, if it was still there. I searched and could not find any specific information about the ruddy thing. It was there during dinner, but when he collected it . . ." Elizabeth shrugged.

"Come to the point, my love," said Harry, not for the first time in his married life.

"You could almost hear him blackmailing as he went on and on. Did she know that the Captain was determined to have her fired? Yes, she did, and thus on and on. Suddenly he switched to Penelope's quarrels with the Captain, and Mrs Gunter spilled all she knew, with the added *bonne bouche* that one day Penelope said 'she would rather see him dead than share him with that bitch' and on another occasion the Captain had his hand 'indelicately placed' upon Penelope! I wonder . . ."

"Honeybody already has and at suitable length."

"He would!" Elizabeth served up the ice-cream and peaches.

Honeybody said: "My grandfather made a note that all communication ceased between Penelope and Mrs Gunter during the course of the Inquest. She removed her belongings to a village near by. It seems that James Fennel was not vindictive: the boys stayed on at school."

"He probably could not cause them to be removed, at any rate without scandal," said Harry.

"In any case," said Honeybody, "he gave them jobs in one of the family businesses when they left school. The old fellow used to say that they had become very wealthy. Mrs Gunter became what we would call a district nurse, very much loved, not a death rattle complete without her presence. She married, a master carpenter with his own shop, when she was sixty-five and lived until long after that."

"I can see that she momentarily panicked at the Inquest—that's what counsel are for. I think she knew something more and deeper." Harry sighed.

"I'll read the diary tonight," said Elizabeth. "And I will spot any fake."

"I think there is some good liqueur overthere," said Honeybody.

III

WITH A STICKY taste in his mouth, and his daughter madly giving him butterfly kisses with her long lashes, at seven a.m. the Inspector for the umpteenth time swore off liqueurs, or at any rate drinking them with Honeybody over some hands of Nap.

At eight fifteen he felt a little better after yoghourt and coffee, averting his gaze from Honeybody's attack upon a long length of salami and his wife's liver and bacon.

"You might poke around on the Mrs Gunter angle," he told Honeybody while his wife was welcoming the daily help, a large stern, capable lady. "I thought I might see Ralf Fennel and the solicitors, still the same, Messrs Snape, Rogers, Tweaking, Dwight Poultry & Son, with several offices all over the county. It was just Snape in 1874, and fortunately the latest Snape, one Gerald, heads the Firm from Greymouth. Sir Charles uses him for personal business, his professional bods being highflyers in Mayfair. I'll see him first thing."

Harry telephoned the Chief Constable, Colonel Angel, who was amiable. "Charlie Fennel's a good chap," he said, "one of the stalwarts, backs us up solidly—he's on the Watch Committee and sees we get our fair financial whack. The lady is earnest, and one wishes she was Mabel or something, but very kind-hearted. Not a penniless old widow exists in a radius of twenty miles who is not persecuted by her ladyship or her myrmidons. Keeps on at them to avoid meat—to benefit their liver and kidneys, y' know—and eat yoghourt and beans. The old ones say it gives them wind, a kind of stalemate and bad feeling. Still, she has 'em taken to the cinema once a week. Yes, Snape is the great-grandson of the chap who cooked up Penny Fennel's defence: 'you perhaps have noticed that like all great defences it was entirely negative. The present one... nobody listening, heh?"

"A direct line, sir, with nobody in the room."

"I suppose his great-grandfather might have been like him. A bit of a sadist. He does our petty-sessional work: I must say that he has the highest proportion of convictions in summary hearing of anybody. But he rather loves it you know, leads them on, sweet as sugar, bland smiles etcetera, and suddenly you see his little mouth water. Then, bang-bang, he shoots them down and enjoys it. I may say that he does not *need* the work, just savours it."

The Chief Constable, Harry realised, was one of those Establishment figures who thought that carnal pleasures should not be enjoyed, and certainly should not be lucrative to persons socially accepted.

"Would you elaborate on that, sir, I think you might be a little coy."

Colonel Angel snorted with laughter. "That would be the day! This is not for Sir Charles, of course, but our Mr Snape is a bit of a creep, although a shrewd one. His ancestor handled the Penelope Fennel case with consummate skill, though it was touch-and-go even with a local jury. My predecessor was impaled by the whole thing. It was Snape who insisted on the Inquest being carried on with. The Chief wanted it to be adjourned and the matter chucked over to the Director of Public Prosecutions and a London jury. She might have swung, you know. But Snape said 'no', it having gone so far in the Press as to prejudice his client's case, which of course it had done. The Coroner had had a hard time to find a jury, nearly everybody qualified being beholden to Jimmy Fennel in one way or another. As it was every man-jack of them must have realised that they were discussing the great big local boss's sister and one day they might want a bank overdraft or credit from the local grain merchants."

"My Sergeant's grandfather, name of Honeybody, was stationed here and accompanied your predecessor to his first interview with Miss Penelope."

There was a burst of laughter. "What we should call today a rare old stud, with a penchant for arresting on suspicion the only person who could not have done it—in bed with a broken spine or something similar. A mighty trencherman and drinker. I alighted on his personal file when I was looking things up for Charlie Fennel. Yet in his way he ran a very good sub-district, on the sexual-transgression, haystack-burning, pinching level. He knew everybody. Faced with anything big—country-house robberies were the things in those days—he went to pieces and snapped up the village idiot. Ah, well, is the present generation better?"

"I think so. A very shrewd man is my Honeybody, wits sharpened on hard city streets."

"I wouldn't gainsay his ancestor's opinion," said Colonel Angel. "It seemed to me that he rather liked the particular bird—buxom, high-coloured, hard-riding—but that he had no doubt that jealousy drove her to it. Bradstreet was a creature of the times, you know, some of the older chaps at the club heard it from their papas. The county were rather proud of their fencibles, a hard-living, devil-may-care lot, straight out of Charles Lever, maybe Thackeray. Not quite 'the thing' like the Household Cavalry or the Foot Guards, younger sons mostly, a little impecunious and tarnished around the gold braid, but good soldiers. Make no mistake about the fencible regiments, they provided at least a cadre of officers who in time of war—the Crimean springs to mind—volunteered for overseas service, foolish fellows. They were a bit raffish, but in those days, when Trade was considered low, it offered an occupation for a quote gentleman unquote with a few hundred a year. The Regimental Balls offered a nice market in girls with good dowries: after they married they generally dropped out and bought a little property."

"I'm a bit confused about the Fennels. I thought Sir Charles and his son were the remaining issue, but there is apparently one Ralf, with an F."

"Oh, Ralf with an F is quite well known, one of the few men whose appearance can empty a club smoking-room. The bore of bores. He was a desert rat was Ralf with an F. He's a remote cousin, the family having more or less lost touch. Charles' father, old William, the nephew incidentally of Penelope, took a fancy to him when he bowled up. Today he is Managing Director of their local food-processing plant. It sells its stuff through the family chain of supermarkets, but even with a captive market Ralf is known to be smart and hard. In fact Charles has intervened occasionally on the part of the local farmers. You know the process: seed, hire of machinery, fertiliser all provided. You contribute land and labour at a contract price. When ripe the produce is first processed in mobile units. I must say you get prime produce, but there is some prejudice among the farmers. I don't know that Ralf would be of any help, but he's a gossip and sometimes their furry ears pick up something ours do not."

Harry thanked him and hung up.

He helped Honeybody unload the car of beer and stout, refused a hundred-item list—or so it seemed—of stuff to be purchased for the children ("In my day, my mamma was not everlastingly flying to the chemist to buy cans of creamed muck") and went to see Mr Snape, who inhabited a delightful old Queen Anne building at the back of the squat, early Victorian Cathedral.

Somehow the Inspector had the impression of a burly, bullying old solicitor, all serge and purple veins. In fact Snape seemed in his middle thirties, slightly built, remarkably sallow, but with rather piercing, close-set emerald-coloured eyes. A disconcerting man, thought Harry.

He sat massaging one thin white hand with the other. "I may say," he said in a husky little voice, "that Sir Charles told me he was engaging you, which is why I am seeing you of course. However, the point is that my great-grandfather acted as solicitor for Miss *Penelope* Fennel, and it is always difficult to decide whether we should divulge information to a collateral descendant or whether it should remain buried in a dusty cupboard. Oh, I'm quite serious: people do not want frivolous solicitors. I was impelled to take counsel from an elder colleague. I must say my original advice to Charles was to have this wretched diary edited, footnoted and published—I understand you can pay for this service if necessary. However, what do *you* want?"

"Did your ancestor think she was guilty?"

He got a sallow smile of genuine amusement. "My ancestor never talked about his cases, but of course he kept the voluminous journals they were so fond of. I suppose," he dangled his secret knowledge in the air, smiling as though it was something tangible, "that after all these years..."

The Inspector said, "It seems a harmless pursuit. After all Sir Charles intends to take up your deceased client from her criminological grave, dust her, refurbish her and restore her honour via Messrs Gollancz or another publisher."

"Well put," Mr Gerald Snape chuckled. "Do you recall

Patrick Hastings' remark? A witness said that she wanted her honour restored. Hastings said that as long as she persisted in having intercourse with old gentlemen on lounge-room sofas the matter was very difficult."

"I must say I do not quite *get* Miss Penelope."

"Do we ever, my dear fellow, and you and I share the same professional interest in human nature? You hear that this or that novelist can peer into people. Damned nonsense. I—and I dare say you—have heard 'em by the hour trotting out their dirty little secrets, but as to what makes 'em tick..." Gerald Snape shrugged elegant little shoulders. "But the only information I really have concerns the governess, Mrs Gunter. She had the goods on Bradstreet."

"My God!"

"At the time when Miss Penelope had trouble with Bradstreet's demands regarding the marriage settlement, she fell into a rage. She suspected he might have huge debts. In fact he had not, just a general insolvency, as one might say, but common enough among his social circle. She said as much to Mrs Gunter. This lady was born locally, daughter of a Frenchman who taught drawing and languages at private schools, a scholar down in the world, ill paid as that kind of thing was in those days. He married a daughter of a local pot-house keeper who died in childbirth. The daughter was well educated by the father, who died in his forties. She married a school-teacher who got work in London and died of typhoid. She had exactly nineteen pounds in the world and no kin. Except that her father had tutored James Fennel in commercial French, so it fell out that James put the children to school and engaged her at one hundred and fifty pounds per year—generous terms—as a companion to his sister. She was a dark little lady with glasses.

"However she was worldly wise and she proposed hiring

an enquiry agent. If you know enough social history, Inspector, you got into a kind of world in 1874 that would curdle Graham Greene's blood. There was, however, a Mr Portman, an ex-police officer who was among the best and in fact years later gave evidence against Oscar Wilde in a very damaging way. He was the first agent ever to secrete himself under a bed, key-holes being the accepted thing before and susceptible of damaging cross-examination. But the Victorian juries fairly lapped up bed springs, though Marshall Hall once got away with it on the suggestion of a violent turn of indigestion, causing cramp and writhing. However it was Mrs Gunter who did the in-between work and Bradstreet got to know it."

"Blackmail?"

"Probably not, but once Bradstreet got into the Cottage Gunter went packing and she knew it. But murder . . . that is a big step, particularly as she was a quiet, amiable soul. You can get into a messy business without connivance, as *we* find all the time. From the record—no, you cannot have it, I'm giving you an expert précis—Bradstreet was madly in love with his mistress, Ursula was her name. Portman was rather too good, I'm afraid, and indiscreet, which left it rather back in my great-grandpapa's lap. He got Gunter in: told her that there was no point in proclaiming that Bradstreet was the father of two illegitimate children by Ursula. I imagine that he realised that harbingers of black news are liable to get a swift decapitation. He edited the report to the effect that Bradstreet had a mistress with whom he was still cohabiting."

"No mention at the Inquest?"

"I would not say this to anybody else except a fellow solicitor or yourself, but the Enquiry posed difficulty. My ancestor bit his nails and saw James Fennel in confidence. The upshot was that Mr Portman and his confidential clerk were sent on an errand to Australia, quite a task in those days, for two thousand pounds. It was a cod, of course, but it took eighteen months. I suppose it was a dubious transaction, but I gather the ancestor considered his duty, plus his remuneration, was tied up with the family. You must remind yourself of the probable effect on an all-male Victorian jury of a private detective investigating male morals. They would have found Penelope guilty of anything."

"I must say," said the Inspector, "that although Penelope was the undeniable front runner, Mrs Gunter seems to have cantered along just behind."

"Somehow," said Snape, massaging his bald, brown skull, "nobody at the time seemed to have terribly much suspicion of her, including James Fennel. There was probably some resentment at her evidence against Miss Penelope, but it was never seriously alleged that she committed the crime. And of course the reason can only be one thing—her personality. She was a mannish, unattractive-looking person, but she was apparently sweet. A faithful friend, a devoted nurse, well known among the gentry and the neighbourhood's poor, a kind of walking Village Institute. I don't think she could be blamed for not standing up against Sir Edmund Socket, whose cross-examination, even in those days, was a disgrace to the Bar. He could not have got away with it anywhere but in a Coroner's court as then constituted. Well, now you know nearly as much as I do."

"Nearly?"

Snape gave his neat little smile.

"Oh, well, you fellows never come completely clean, I guess. I'm off to see Ralf Fennel, never having met him."

"I would not think much information—apart from military matters and 'Our 'arbour' will be forthcoming: a loquacious fellow, though as it happens the only Fennel alive besides Charles, his wife and their son. Two world wars fairly wiped them out. There was a brother of the 'original' Fennel who went to Australia. It's a boom-and-burst country as you know, or was up to 1939. Their fortunes reflected it. Ralf was quite well educated, but in 1939 he was an orphan running the small family farm in New South Wales. He sold up and joined the Army. Charles' father was William Fennel, fours years old at the time Bradstreet died. Ralf called in at the end of the war—the two sides of the family had been without contact for seventy years." Snape shrugged. "Today it's difficult to preserve continuity over twelve thousand miles, more so in those days when a letter might take two months. William had a strong family sense, but in any event took a shine to Ralf, making him a director of two of his companies. He is now managing the local food plant. For all his garrulousness, he knows his job. The family farm was geared to food-canners so he knows it inside out."

"Married?" asked Harry with the idle but insatiable curiosity of a policeman.

"No," said Snape. "He lives in a very very nice little house not far from here. William Fennel left it to him in his Will plus twelve thousand pounds. I suppose he would get about three thousand as Managing Director. He lives quietly, belongs to a few clubs where he is the resident bore. Now I come to think of it, there was a time when he was assiduous in the pursuit of family history, as a lot of his race are when visiting the Old Dart as he insists on calling it. Does he mean Dartmoor?"

"Not in the prison sense. It's a term of endearment and I don't think the prison was operating for civilians when the first lot of cons were shipped over. Dartmoor was a P.O.W.

camp you know, a Georgian Belsen but rather worse, God bless our inventive minds."

"Well," said Snape, meditatively, "you might get something out of him, but take your earplugs."

Ralf might be garrulous, but he was almost certainly efficient. Long experience of such visitations had made Harry a pretty fair judge, and the small, dark man presided behind a clear desk, flanked with three telephones, an intercom, and a tape-recorder. The Inspector had been asked to go in at once by the pretty middle-aged secretary in the anteroom.

"I met one of your men last night," said Ralf amiably, "a good old sweat, salt of the earth but always complaining, if I'm any judge."

This would have to be stopped short: the Chief Inspector recognised the road to Tobruk looming up fast.

"I believe you know something of the English branch of the Fennels."

"Scots and proud of it. Even in Australia we married Scots. Charles is the first Fennel to marry a Gentile," he cackled. "I suppose we haven't got too much interest in family back home, on account of some of the ripe specimens you sent us from time to time: and Mary Gilmore superintended the burning of the convict records in 1901—a lot of the society bods used to blush when they met that nice lady. But yes, I did go through his own archives: in fact Charles got me to dig out the relevant documents of 1874. Trying, very, because Lady Fennel is a leetle intense about it. And I've got something on my conscience." Portentously, he opened a drawer and extracted a small yellowing piece of paper with a regimental crest. The writing was bold, but rather unformed. It said: "Dear Mrs Fennel, In view of the circumstances I think that in future we should meet only on most formal terms. Believe me, with every good wish, yours truly, Oswald Bradstreet." It was dated June tenth, a week before the announcement of the engagement.

"I took the liberty of suppressing this from Charles and Lady Fennel. I mean, it looks like a chunk of rather dirty washing. It was between the leaves of the day-book that James' wife used: one of those locked affairs. I was very cryptic: you will see that from what she wrote she gave the Superintendent down from the Yard 'every help', which means she tried to have her sister-in-law hung—nice lady, but there! James Fennel was a stuffy dog, you know, and his wife was ten years younger and very beautiful. She never got on with Penelope, who was the same age.

"I asked Charles how his grandmother and grandfather got on: his reply was that their married life had been a little stormy. They never mentioned Penelope to him, though his father had told him about the case because there were occasional hack articles in the popular press."

"Any theories?" The Chief Inspector tucked the paper into his wallet.

Ralf clasped his hands behind his head. "I'd stick a little wager on suicide, although why he did not use cyanide, which was quite readily obtainable, or a bullet is difficult to explain. Still, it might have been easiest to come by, and probably he knew nothing of the effects. The denial that he had taken anything was purely a reflex, and, such is the nature of the poison, he might even have thought he was recovering."

"There were his accusatory words to Penelope, that she had done wrong..."

"Reviving their running quarrel: her suspicion about his private life. You know, Inspector, the last half of the nineteenth century fascinates me and I have read a great deal on the subject. Keeping your head above water was a first principle, because if you sank, you went down fast and nobody cared much. I would guarantee that Bradstreet's financial affairs were worse than ever came out. I doubt he could have clung on to his commission for long. Then, it might have meant a job as an 'estate manager' or else hanging round the City taking directorships in shady companies or perhaps becoming a social secretary. I wondered... I got an old pamphlet on the Regiment. They had a fund, of about eighteen thousand pounds, left to them by some old local fire-eater in Napoleonic times. For relieving distress among troops' families. It did cross my mind that maybe..." he rubbed thumb and forefinger. "I came across a note to James dated a month before his death, postponing a dinner date because he had to approve the accounts of the Regimental Fund. So you see... We got a great many men of the Captain's stamp in Australia at that time—remittance men—and mostly they sank. My dad used to say you could see them thick as flies around Carlton and Fitzroy, where the cheaper rooming houses were, cracked shoes, shiny pants, cheap restaurants and the pubs. He could have embezzled and taken the handy way out."

"You should have been the detective," said Harry. "Well, we'll see."

The *Greymouth Recorder* was in a dusty little square. There was a sound of a platen machine somewhere in the basement fulfilling the legend "jobbing printing executed".

There was a bright, mini-skirted young lady behind the dusty counter.

"Can I see your file for 1874?"

"If it hasn't fallen to bits: it seems very popular. Are you in the trade?"

"Journalist? No, I'm here on holiday."

She gave him a saucy look of unbelief but fetched the black-bound broadsheet-sized file. In 1874 the *Recorder* ran to eight or twelve pages of eight point, occasionally, in its interminable list of persons attending weddings, funerals or the mass of functions from darts matches to bellringers' outings, sliding down into six point. The front page was purely advertisements, and the headings squat, black and one column wide.

The *Recorder* (the Chief Inspector's fancy conjured up the anxious wagging of beards in the boardroom) had played the Bradstreet Inquest straight.

**ENQUIRY INTO
DEATH OF CAPTAIN**
Seated with a jury at the Grey Goat on
Thursday the death of Captain Oswald
Bradstreet was enquired into by the
Deputy Coroner.

This set the pace and even so the prolix reporting of Victorian provincial newspapers was missing. In those days the paper came out on Wednesday—the Inquest having dragged on for five days—so staleness as well as sychophancy might have accounted for the ruthless summarising of the leading evidence.

But this he had expected. Even today few small-town editors, except ones going bankrupt and not caring anyhow, go out of their way to offend their fellow burgesses at the Constitutional Club.

Starting at the first date in January, he worked steadily through, ignoring the quizzical glances of the girl. The Regiment had been much concerned with social life and military occasions, providing guards of honour, marches past, demonstrations, and almost monthly balls. His eyes ached slightly at the list of names. Once or twice he saw "Colonel Chuck's party"; among the names listed appeared that of Miss Penelope Fennel.

There was no mention of Captain Bradstreet's funeral: he remembered that somehow old Sir Ferguson Bradstreet had got him into the family vault on the sold estates in Derbyshire.

By the end of July Bradstreet must have been interred, but by reason of the doggedness which his kind of work induced in every good policeman he plodded on. For two months the Regiment retired from dances, resuming with an October Gala. He turned to December.

Suddenly his scalp twitched:

FUNERAL OF MAJOR BULL

The late Major John Paul Bull of the Regiment, son of the late Robert and the late Hyacinth Bull, formerly of Delhi, was interred yesterday in the churchyard of St. Botolph's, the Rev. Phipp conducting the service.

A small item, but rather significant. There were no lists, of mourners at the church, of those at the graveside, or the remorseless compilation of those who attended the "cold collation and refreshment" which should have followed. Neither were the undertakers, pall-bearers and other dismal dignitaries listed. He double-checked on other funerals. Yes, it was most unusual.

He beckoned to the young lady. "Could you tell me the date your local Fencible Regiment packed up? I mean, it is important to me." Two one-pound notes dangled between his fingers.

"You are offensive! I'm a journalist."

"I've read you cannot be bribed."

"You said you're not: and you're not a writer, they haven't got two quid. And I must say, barring the stunted growth, you could be a copper."

"Think of Chas. Dickens, he got loaded with lolly."

"You need a beard for that. All right, but go and have a cuppa. There's a lousy old handwritten index compiled by generations of sozzled journalists when it was quiet around the place." But she said it with a quiet kind of pride.

The Chief Inspector spent half an hour prowling around the boutiques around the little square, flinching at the prices. To his surprise when he went back the file which was opened was dated July, 1875, itemising over two pages the military history (rather thin and high-spotted by the rounding-up of twenty Frenchmen near Dover in 1806, they alleging they had landed by mistake in a heavy fog) and the social prowess (great) of the Regiment, which now by the wisdom of the War Office was being disbanded under new schemes of Reform. Their last Colonel, Chuck by name, scion of the well-known local family, took the March Past.

"Reform, Thou Goddess to whom we all must bow with thine hand-maidens of gas, of steam, of electricity and improved cloth production, Thou must pardon a small tear that trickles down the cheek of this chronicler as he thinks of bygone glories, exclaiming *EHEU FUGACES*." With this flourish the Regiment disappeared from history and the pages of the *Greymouth Recorder*. Harry thanked the girl and left before she could argue about the box of chocolates he pushed over.

Elizabeth was glowing over the efficiency of the daily woman and the fact that the chops were better than you could get in London—or perhaps it was the sweet air coming through the windows—and Honeybody had written a thousand words of reportage for the Chief Inspector to revise.

The twins had fortunately been fed and placed in the playpen, watched by Mr Bones, who curiously never knew quite what to make of them, though he had never been unsure about Amanda. After all, the Chief Inspector would sometimes say, he should be used to seeing young people in litters, a remark unappreciated by his wife.

For a change it was peaceful, everything cooked to time, the soufflé a success (sometimes they were not), Amanda nattering about the first cow she had consciously seen and Honeybody quietly gloating over the prospect of a night's boozing. Afterwards his wife decided to take the car to look at the town, and Honeybody volunteered to look after the three kids while he dozed in the little walled garden at the back of the house, once doubtless used for herbs but now pleasantly over-run. Amanda helped him take out a deck chair.

When the house was quiet eventually Harry drew his first drink of the day and lazed upon a day bed. Eventually he shook his head and propped himself against the back rest. The telephone and its guide were within an outstretched hand. It was no coincidence, for in country towns families linger on. There was a Professor John Chuck, at Stargable House, Rushton Lane. He went and found the map among his papers. He thought it might be half an hour's walk. He showered, changed, scribbled a note to his wife, ascertained that Honeybody and the twins were comatose and that Amanda was trying to tie wildflowers on the dog's tail and went out, walking peacefully along lanes only slightly disfigured by petrol fumes and massacred hedgerows.

It was more than half an hour before he dawdled up to Stargable House, having first to find it among the thickly growing trees and undergrowth of its three acres. With its unkemptness and high perpendicular lines it might have been some rotting old spacecraft in an alien landscape.

The front door was open—he was to find it generally was, there being nothing pinchable in the house—and through it came a curious, spine-tickling sound, rather like the slack stringed fiddle used by the Arabs. And there were words screeched in hoarse old voices, old archaic words:

"Anum, scanum, diddle um danum
Down to sacrifice goes we."

Peering round, he saw that there was a small hall, a conceit based upon all Great Halls. About the parquet floor capered a fat old dame in her sixties and a truly ancient old fellow in a smock, the latter being extraordinarily nippy and his thin legs twinkling.

Posturing in the corner, in tights and ballet shoes was, yes, it was the girl he had seen in the newspaper office, rehearsing as it were the capering. The noise was emanating from a curious, ancient instrument held by an elderly man who looked like a cockatoo, with tufted white hair setting off a noble hooked nose below snapping black eyes. Next to him, on a stool, was an amiable-looking man of roughly similar age who looked like a small scrubbed pig.

The cockatoo waved his odd-looking bow in a gesture to indicate a break.

"They'll pay through the nose for this, sir," cackled the ancient man, stopping as he saw Harry.

"I'm looking for Professor John Chuck."

"I am he," said the cockatoo, with great dignity shelving his instrument, "and this is my brother, the eminent Antiquarian and Archaeologist. Oh, and my niece, Charlotte." The girl bobbed. The Chief Inspector wondered why she looked frightened.

"Professor . . ."

"For many years," said John Chuck, in his wobbly basso, "I was professor of the clarinet. Now I do not use the title on informal occasions."

It was rather like Queen Victoria inviting John Brown to call her Vicky.

"He was prowling round the office this morning on a flimsy excuse. I think he is a policeman."

"I thought *you* were a journalist."

She looked defenceless, yet aggressive, and amazingly pretty. A luscious nineteen, Harry thought.

"I'm being trained mornings," she said, "office-girl stuff at the moment."

"A respect of the law is the integral in the growth of civilisation," squeaked the ex-archaeologist and antiquary. "But come, a, um, perhaps a glass of port?"

The girl looked uneasy, but trotted towards what was perhaps the passageway to a kitchen. Looking round, the Chief Inspector saw that the hall was ingeniously furnished, what there was of it, with chairs and tables made from the sturdier class of packing case, uneasily disguised with plastic secured by drawing-pins.

He accepted a chair, not uncomfortable because of a

chunk of plastic foam strategically situated, while the two brothers flanked him. Surprisingly quickly the girl returned. The biscuits were good, the wine a Marsala of a class the Inspector had never experienced, but on the low end of the scale. She flushed and looked at him imploringly.

"A very sound vintage," he managed to mutter, and Professor Chuck nodded condescendingly. He turned to where the ancient man and the woman were standing.

"I think that's all, Mr and Mrs Tubb, no good overdoing it."

"I'll keep Tubb 'otted up with vigorous applications of liniment," said Mrs Tubb.

"And a drop of whisky for the toobs," said her husband with finality.

"We—that is I and my brother—do not—being men of the spirit—knew about vinous things, but when we get worldly-wise visitors we like to extend our best," said the porcine brother complacently.

Harry listened to the tap of the Tubbs' footsteps die away. "I am a policeman—on holiday—by name of Harry James. I have been employed by Sir Charles Fennel to assist him in a history of the Fennel family, my usefulness being non-literary but a capacity for tracking down and checking relevant facts. You may phone him..." He realised that there could scarcely be a phone..."or better still I could have him send you round a note. It is about the old Fencible Regiment that was stationed here and disbanded nearly one hundred years ago. The last Colonel..."

"Was our grandfather, and Charlotte's great," said the Professor.

"Its history intertwines with that of Greymouth," said Harry, "and that is my pigeon," he added vaguely. "I wondered whether the Colonel had left any papers."

"He did," squeaked the porcine brother, "and of little value as he retraced so much that you can find more stirringly depicted in so many other MSS, Regimental histories, etcetera. Interesting, maybe, to a Greymouth resident, but of no publishing or antiquarian interest except a few details of Mess procedure. All gone, those shades, all gone. There is only one thing, you know, that a policeman might find of interest..."

"Why did they disband the Regiment?" said Harry.

"Precisely, and you may have apprehended that it was, as one understands the business term to be, a forced sale, and diplomatically a larger event burying a scandalous event by its magnitude, like Munich. However you are wrong in thinking that we do not keep a telephone. We do if only because our niece is of a generation bound with telephone wires, but we bar incoming calls because Charlotte is frequently about her business and John and I, who am Paul, incidentally, can be about *our* studies. So we had it put, with studied reluctance by the telephone undertaking, in the coal hole."

"Over here," said the girl, advancing to the huge fireplace in which crouched a rather battered gas fire, of the kind which includes an imitation yule log in ruby glass. By its side was a knob which she twisted and pulled, and a disguised three-feet-square door opened. In the blackness Harry could discern a hand-set.

"In years gone by," said the Professor, "and so that the company should not be disturbed, coal was stoked through from the outer wall of the house, so that the appropriate servitor could enter the hall, open the hatch and renew the flames with coal or perhaps logs. The door is thick and sound-proofed with cork, so that the instrument may ring and ring with no disturbance to our labours. My brother, the more practical of us, thought of it."

Harry squatted painfully: it was certainly only used by the agile niece. Sir Charles was out, but her ladyship was in. He explained the business and not daring merely to beckon, stood up, cradling the instrument, summoning the Professor with a half-bow. The old gentleman listened with a kind of crouched unction, murmured a few words and finally handed the telephone back to the Chief Inspector, who made the appropriate noises before hanging up.

"Let us see, when was it we dined with the Fennels?"

"Before Christmas," said Paul, practically, "she wanted some advice about the private chapel."

The Professor looked at Harry with his disconcerting eyes: "She has some plan for restoring it to its former grandeur. The earlier Fennels, having turned to the Church of England, did it with pomp, my dear sir, and two resident chaplains, though one of them was expected to do something about their extensive greenhouses. Although," a thought gripped the Professor, "being an American, can she partake of our Communion?"

"Naturalised by marriage, no doubt," said Harry, "thence eligible."

The girl stood back watching him with her fox-like eyes, face studiously blank.

"Ah, the Law can always find a way," murmured the Professor, and Harry could have sworn that he was about to putter away into some other room had not his porcine brother held his sleeve.

"Inspector," said the Antiquary, "I perpend you are after—if my reading of Miss Sayers has not misled me upon the technical word—the motive why Major John Bull committed suicide with cyanide in brandy—quite out of

Nicholas Nickleby. You remember how the master invoked that smell of almonds in the dirty police cab? It was at the end of October with the spirit of Christmas coming up. Bear with me, you shall presently have the original diary. Our grandfather, Colonel Chuck, describes Bull as a hard-drinking (brandy) disciplinarian and rider to hounds who ranked as popular in the county. His origins were obscure, but Indian Army—a long way away then, his father having died as a subaltern in some frontier skirmish ... all those bones lying around ... and his mother dying of fever. Hm. In due course he married a little lady, daughter of a superior farmer or decayed gent, what ye will, with eight thousand pounds and a tiny property, some years younger than Bull. Apparently with his drink and his horses, and one dares to say whist, Bull pretty well went through that. He was Administrator of the Regimental Fund. Captain Bradstreet," Paul Chuck's little blue eyes ogled the Chief Inspector for a long second, "was honorary Auditor. Briefly, twelve thousand was embezzled from the Fund. Bradstreet's successor, a very careful and conscientious man—unlike, it must be said, most of his fellows—discovered it in the September. Bull procrastinated, but on October the fourth was found dead in his office with a brandy glass with cyanide lacing the spirit. Now our grandfather was a man of a type which one hardly believes exists today. The Regiment's honour was his honour. First, he had the Regimental Surgeon certify the death as due to Apoplexy and saw that Bull was interred without fuss. He even sent a firing party after praying for six solid hours for guidance, but took care that it was as small a funeral as possible. Then he immediately replaced the twelve thousand pounds. Times were bad—though as unworldly fellows in the book-keeping sense it seems to my brother and me that times are always bad when you want to sell something. But against all advice he sold what he had to raise the twelve thousand."

Paul looked around the room.

"It ruined us," he squeaked, "taking, as it were, the working capital. This did not satisfy Grandfather. He went up to the Horse Guards and told them exactly what had happened, thus setting off, like a mechanical toy, the Establishment. That illogical young person," he stabbed a paw towards Charlotte, "talks of an Establishment. Well, not she," he softened, "but those friends of hers. They don't know what an Establishment is. The Queen was consulted. It was settled that the Regiment should be discreetly disbanded and that my grandfather should retire. He was fifty-four and lived another twenty-eight years. He had married late and his bride died young. We can only remember him through his works—as an honourable gentleman."

"I do not think you should talk to him, there may be something ulterior. Don't forget, once a policeman always one," said Charlotte, raising and dropping one disconcertingly shapely leg.

"My girl," said the Inspector, shamelessly voyeuring, lusciously and rashly voyeuring, he realised as his back creaked after the telephone effort, "the Victorian habit of thrashing children should be revived. However, if you wish to be a journalist you will find that you often rely upon the police. I do not mean only crime stuff, far from it, but almost any story. The local cops know what goes on and where the places are. They co-operate, perhaps at lower levels for a packet of fags. But if it gets around that you are ... politely non-acceptable, then you can whistle for your newsy supper. That's a bit of advice which will take you far."

(Like that glorious bum, he thought.)

Harry turned to the two brothers. "You of course know

that the implication is that Major Bull murdered Captain Bradstreet."

Professor Chuck was stroking the strange stringed instrument. Suddenly he looked rather different. "Although I confess that we are, in the modern term, broke to the wide, we are not without honour, my dear sir. Our grandfather, and Charlotte's great, was no country hick. Everything was swept under the carpet, and my grandfather, broken and ruined, retired here to his collection of lead soldiers."

"I would like to have a sight of the original, not that I doubt your précis is correct."

The Professor had picked up the stringed instrument and was looking at it as if he had never seen it before. "But just what is your interest, Mr James?"

The Chief Inspector made a decision. "I do not suppose it is earth-shattering, but I would not consider myself able to reveal it without the trust in your discretion that I have."

It usually worked; the brothers looked sepulchral but the girl sceptical. He gave her a cold eye. You could not expect an old head on young shoulders, but the unofficial part of him registered the fact that she did have bits more effective than wisdom.

"In the family history that Lady Fennel is compiling, the matter of the great-aunt, Penelope, is necessarily to be taken into consideration. You may remember..."

"Yes indeed," squeaked brother Paul. "It is years, really, since poisoning became unpopular, around 1911 in fact. It was, one supposes, almost the only weapon left to some ladies before," he looked at Charlotte, "they stopped wearing stays and went about unchaperoned. That year marked the end of it all, though it started in the nineties with the telephone operators. Women are so much more dexterous: I used to have them on my 'digs'."

"She done it," said Charlotte, waggling her left leg. "Pure case of jealousy as I read it, so the mad creature slipped him a shot of poison. Poor lady, as if a man is worth hanging for."

"My dear," said brother Paul, "jealousy and its handsisters, self-abnegation and mother love, are the glory of womanhood, the true inspiration of poet and dramatist. Take..."

"My girl friends don't think that way," said Charlotte. "We abnegated far too long."

"For the birds in fact, if you accept thirtyish slang," said Harry. He was rewarded by a steady, unpleasant look. Maybe the girl would make a journalist at that.

"You mean that Major Bull poisoned him, placing the deadly fluid in his pocket flask?" said the Professor, sliding his basso up and down.

"I suppose it is a supposition."

"Funny thing about this fellow Bradstreet," said brother Paul, "but the grandfather reckoned he was a man of small mean economies. We all have them, though I seem to be total, *force majeure*."

"I would not say that," said the Professor.

"Nor would I," declared Charlotte, colours flying, with a fervour which would have impressed the Chief Inspector more if she had had more clothes on. There was a definite sartorial factor in the credibility gap, he realised. It was President Johnson's inability to wear a frock coat that finally got him.

"My dear sir," he hastened, "here am I being entertained handsomely; it is so strange hospitality has no better verb, but that is interesting. The only snag is that the poison gives almost instantaneous stomach pains, though tasteless."

"Grandfather always used to say that Bradstreet had a system to obtain virtually free brandy. In those days no gentleman could refuse a request to fill a visitor's hip flask for the ride home. An English pint is twenty ounces and a good hip flask could hold twelve. Three times a day meant one-and-a-half bottles, a gentleman's allowance, though it was around three and six per bottle, more if *fine champagne*, which had come in commercially at that time. I would say that the Regiment perhaps drank Rémy Martin as a matter of course, and that point is that if Captain Bradstreet *emptied* his daily gains into bottles, rather like today we empty inferior Scotch into expensive container," said brother Paul, jerked back to reality, "then the poison could have come from anybody. Nothing easier, I fear."

"Only the time factor, sir," said the Chief Inspector. "He refilled his flask at the Cottage."

"Only one?"

"What are you saying?" The chair creaked ominously under Harry.

"There were two," said brother Paul. "They came in pairs from that place in London. One for the hip, t'other, sometimes for cherry brandy or suchlike, for the breast pocket of your outer coat. The grandfather rather envied 'em, Penelope not having spared money and having had them handworker. He specifically mentions 'a pair of flasks'."

"My God," said Harry, "then anybody could have poisoned him. I wonder..."

He checked himself, no need to wonder. An astute defence, presenting only a dead bat to the Coroner's Inquest, would have kept that in reserve against a possible trial. Among the items which comprised the Captain's dress was a formal jacket. He remembered the type of flask, a very slim one as against its fatter partner to be worn against the rump.

After all, why delve further? This, suitably written up (he depended upon Elizabeth's literary touches in his reports), must surely result in a plump bonus from the good knight. There was only one more question to be asked.

"Why didn't your grandpa give evidence about the two flasks—much was made of the fact that he had one filled at the Cottage."

"He was a simple man," squeaked Paul after some thought. "The diary—I will dig it out, have it wrapped up and delivered—sums that up admirably. He came to the conclusion that if he did anything it might complicate the situation, and of course at that time he could not preview John Bull's suicide. If it comes to that, the fact that the Captain carried two flasks was obviously common knowledge around the Regiment."

The Chief Inspector thanked them and departed. On the way home the not unpleasant whine of a buzz-saw, sunk as it were into the soft cushion of late afternoon and the heavy air, made him glance at, yes that was what the strange lettering on the thatched barn said, "Cryer's Creations. Stranger Abandon Soap."

The wardrobe in which the diary was found had been delivered (*vide* Lady Fennel's earnest imparting) to the skilled hands of one Jasper Cryer. Harry turned off the laneway and walked up the gravelled pathway to the barn. The inside was darkish, a peculiarity of old carpentry shops, but the company was not. Even in the half-light, with resinous air tickling his lungs, the Chief Inspector was taken aback, for there were racks upon racks of Victorian whatnots, those strange pieces of wood, puzzling in character, designed to rest hats from Royal Garden Parties, Moustache Cups, small target pistols for father's vendetta against the rats in the cellar, and, frankly, God knew what about a whatnot except the owner. A very tall man, about thirty, and a very tall girl were sticking purple-dyed ostrich feathers on one of them, cruciform shaped and inset with artificial pearls.

"Sir, sir, sir," said the tall man, "I'm Cryer and unless my brain is addled we are strangers. Trade or private?"

"You might say I'm neither, merely a temporary employee of Sir Charles, looking into this question of a diary found." Peering around in the darkness he perceived the shattered remains of a huge dark-brown closet.

"That's the job," said Cryer. "This is the wife by the by. She is the brains, I'm the carp. Victoriana is what we make, and all above board. That is you can have this"—he indicated the piece with the inset ostrich feathers—"for eighteen pounds. The wood dates from around 1820, a sideboard I picked up, makes about eighty-four whatnots if cut right. Mind you, what you sell it as, repro. or genuine, is your business. I've heard of two hundred quid being got for the more ghastly ones."

"The Slade," said his wife, who looked as though she might have trouble with nits, "spent a lot of money on training me to recognise the Beautiful. Do you know what I found, the bloody fools will pay for the hidoeus! I was wondering whether a great big gob of green bottle glass would improve this one."

"I wonder whether something worse, say an old imitation pearl handle and, or would that be overdoing it, a bit of human hair glued on. Or would that be too much?" said the Chief Inspector.

"Nothing is too much. Again, while you are hot."

"A thyrsus," said Harry, entranced, "William Morris loved them."

"They must be decent," said Cryer, "because they think their great-grandmas were decent, poor fools, but did you say thyrsus?"

"It's a rod on the top of which is a pine-cone," said the Inspector, "and a symbol of Dionysus."

"Drink!" said Mrs Cryer who, Harry realised, was really lovely under the various layers of grime. "Victorian pas coming home with a skinful and lustful desires, huh?"

"One thinks something of the sort."

"This might be the start of something, Fay," said the carpenter. "Victorian fertility figures. They might outdo the pots, with red roses and little cherubs, which her brother makes for us. We do a coat of arms on the bottom side and sell 'em to the Yankee trade for thirteen pounds each. It's astonishing."

"About Sir Charles' wardrobe..."

"I like making something good in the built-in furniture line. A man does. Something for the present, not like copying the past like every mug with his little Vic. and Bertie handbooks asks you. I've got a free hand for the Fennels and it will be something, perhaps something that will last. This diary was a nothing. I'm taking the 'robe to pieces with loving hands as you might say. *In situ* I had to knock it into four pieces, more roughly than I might have wanted, because Lady Fennel is impatient. Here I take my time, leaf upon leaf, and in one of the little sub-cupboards, if one can use the word, was this diary. I'd 've slung it away only Fay started looking through it—you can sell pages of Victorian diaries as lampshades, but we don't do it—and, well you know as much as I do."

"That puts the cat among the pigeons," decided Elizabeth after the supper things had been washed up by the men.

"The poor bosomy soul, if not framed, was victimised."

"She did apparently commit suicide," said Harry.

"I know how she felt, that time everybody thought I was a murderer."*

"Instead of that you got twins," said Honeybody, sleepily after the smoked haddock and scrambled eggs.

"The lady seems to have several lines of defence," said the Chief Inspector. "First her diary, all ready to be popped out and bosom clasped: second the possible existence of two flasks, although for that matter he might have had half a dozen strewn about. I think I've got two somewhere among the junk. And you know as well as I do that a good way to commit murder is to do it, get yourself arraigned and then be found not guilty."

"But you just commented on her virtual suicide," said Elizabeth.

"A lot of them cannot take it," said Harry, sighing. "The few who can are mad, although I would not let the public know of this. The rest just get this terrible weight on them, it crushes them. Apart from your thug, who is mad, people do not murder twice, and I include among the thugs the Jack the Rippers, Al Capones and the poisoners. The sane person who murders does not do it twice."

"All talk," said Elizabeth. Harry reluctantly nodded agreement.

"Do you think the Chuck brothers are mad?" asked Elizabeth. "And the niece sounds quite brazen. Ballet! An excuse for throwing her legs around."

It was remarkable what twins did to a lady, thought the Chief Inspector while opining that the brothers were merely eccentric and the girl a product of having been brought up apparently by a clarinettist and an antiquary.

* *Some Beasts No More*

"I did get a whiff of what that dancing and yammering might be about, up at the pub. There's an American outfit that buys culture," rumbled Honeybody.

"Buys culture?"

"Slabs of it, copyrights it and lays it away in some Yankee foundation."

"What kind of culture?"

"Not what I'd call Culture," said Honeybody. "Now my dad had Sir John Lubbocks Hundred Best Books, which no working-class family could understand. I had an aunt who was in the Left Book Club and was put in prison for misunderstanding it and biting a policeman, and there was *Cassell's Book of Knowledge* for me. I remember my frustration when at the age of thirteen I looked up 'whore' and found it left out. But they are always on at you about it, book clubs or monthly parts. My father got conned on to Doggies in twelve monthly parts. I bet I know more useless things about dogs than anybody." Mr Bones, his forward parts draped over the good Sergeant's knees, whined and commenced to flea the large midriff which drooped over him.

There was a howling from the room which housed the twins.

"We'll just nick up and check at the pub, dear, and take the dog for his wetting. Bye for now," said Harry.

When "they" were dealing with twins they could not do much in the positive way, thought Harry with satisfaction as they went out to the car with Mr Bones on his lead. Tomorrow there was a baby-sitter arranged and the local theatre, which had no stage as such, was starting a production in which everyone startlingly wore clothes or at worst fig leaves, to which he proposed taking his wife.

It was a nice pub, if anybody ever had the money to drink these days, or the temerity to risk the breath test if driving. It was the one in which the Inquest had been held, pubs in those days generally having one floor, usually occupied by the local glee club, that could raise a fiver per day as a Coroner's Court in season.

As usual Honeybody appeared to have existed there since the fixtures, old, fake stained glass and dutch metal foot-rests, mahogany-stained pine and benches which only the British spines could tolerate.

The landlord smelled police, as good landlords can, and was wary, a pimply-faced man who knew his business.

"I can hear a yodelling kind of noise up above," said the Chief Inspector, shovelling it out straight.

"No dancing, singing or merriment on premises," intoned the landlord, "but the Coroner's Court above is let out to eminently respectable Americans, one being black and written up in the *Sunday Guide* in a suitably waggish patronising way. The dancers, Mr and Mrs Tubb, sir, are a mine of old folk-lore, ancient respectable villagers. He was a Hedger, sir, before rheumatism, when he became the undertaker's mute, but it suddenly cured itself under National Health and the Pension and he is rare nippy, sir, and good as any at capering though I do not allow same in Hours on the Licensed Parts as the local by-law is against such things. The head man is over there refreshing himself on Teachers and Branch Water what I stock specially for him and his party."

The publican was that English curiosity, a semi-educated man who from years of talking down to the totally uneducated and fawning up to the bureaucracy, both brewery and state, which ruled his life had acquired a very odd way of talking, like a faultily plugged switch-board.

"These Americans live here?" asked Harry.

"Gawd, no, wish they did, a plover's-egg omelette job they are, and the food's as good here as you'll get, or the old lady gets it scone-hot from me. But they're mad about bathrooms, specially the black chap, though he should use shoe polish. But, good gracious me, there is no vice in folk-dancing."

Quaint old country customs involving young ladies and unguents made from toadstools lingered in the Chief Inspector's mind as he looked at the American, heard the faint drone of his questioning of a half-witted farming type. The interrogator was built like a grand piano. The trouble with Brooklyn Jews, he realised uneasily, was that they did take culture so seriously, wringing the last drop of blood out of it before presenting the desiccated remains to some museum and the rest to a publisher. He thought they were serious about it from memories of the controversial books it was occasionally his painful duty to help adjudicate upon, flanked by a dismal man from Customs and a Treasury Counsel. Why could not they confine themselves to Commerce or the rag trade, the Chief Inspector wondered uneasily, why this fixation upon Culture which became by extension a kind of itch?

"Billy the Song" was what the American confided, on being introduced by the Publican, as the name by which he was known personally in thirty-seven countries and in four hundred and sixty dialect zones, and eighteen hundred official regions, including all the English counties.

The Chief Inspector asked if he would have a Scotch. "I'm working for Sir Charles Fennel on his family archives," he said.

"Man, there might be a rich lode for us," exclaimed Billy, "and we pay well for a complete quit claim, the foundation requiring all rights. And," he finished his drink, "do we have trouble explaining it to old Indians, etcetera. Complete quittance," he said, "but come upstairs where we have a bottle on expenses always on tap. I just came down here to think. You know how it is?"

"I'd like to take a look," said Harry.

"Confidentially, and I'm always confidential when we have a firm option with two thousand dollars on the line, and one more as maximum payment, this is about old Anglo-Saxon habits. I wish I knew their sexual behaviour better."

"Dirty," said Harry, thinking of the Assize list.

"I sometimes wish that the late Mr Boddingham had left it sexual instead of cultural."

"Boddingham?"

"The Bra King. Two-eighty sizes. If you were human he could fit you, as the ads went. Twenty-seven million bucks he left and no children, he being a purely tit man all his life, but interested in folk-lore: the songs and dances of the peasants. He said that the reason he made so much out of bras and men's corsets was that people did not sing and caper like they ought. He was once thrown out of the Brown Derby—in 1941—for stripping off and prancing. It is the singing, that great, great, folk tradition, which is my perquisite. I guess I have recorded nine thousand originals."

"What happens to them?" Harry was bemused.

"After being registered in the Library of Congress, they are in copyright and this is invested entirely in the Clarence J. Boddingham Foundation."

"The public can't sing 'em if you buy them?"

"Indeed, sir, no, we pay our solicitors, as you would call them, two hundred thousand dollars per year to prevent singing, dancing, or, by a decision of the Supreme Court, humming or jigging, Justice Fortas abstaining."

Mr Bones exhibited some alarm as they climbed the steep staircase. Above came a whining and strumming and clacking. Nasal tones could be presently distinguished:

"Anum, scanum, diddle um danum,
  Down to sacrifice goes we."

He was hardly surprised when in the brilliantly lit room he saw Miss Charlotte was sawing away at the strange, stringed instrument that he had seen that afternoon manipulated by her uncle. Madly capering were the couple referred to as Mr and Mrs Tubb. As he watched they gave one further howl and subsided, both making towards a small table with bottles on it.

A ferrety man switched off an expensive recording apparatus, and another carrying a document came from the shadows.

"Any more like this?" he said.

"Two dozen more, maister"—the old man was hamming it, thought the Chief Inspector, and those gaiters were clearly recently and inexpertly made.

"Don't 'e dew it, Tubb," howled the old lady. "Think of the curse."

"Now, my dears," said the black American in his cultivated Washington accent, "rid your minds of superstition and witchcraft. You have been intoning and dancing out a fertility rite, of Saxon origin, but probably fifteenth century because the design of that instrument (though not of course its making) is Arabic brought back by the Crusaders."

"Fertility," said the old man, rinsing his gums with whisky, "that's sex, ennit? I always said it has to be double pay with sex. Stands to reason, the wife being a decent lady and always praised at the Village Institute for it. Say five thousand dollars."

"Now, grandad, we made it quite clear that three thousand five hundred is top."

"That was all right about the fruit-picking," said the

ancient man, "and the sin-eatin' and pagan rituals in the old meadow, but now you're talking sex. Callin' up the Devil don't mean much, my family being on familiar terms like."

"Don't say it, Cuthbert," impored his wife.

"And there is an antique stringed instrument," said Charlotte in her high clear voice, and Billy the Song grinned.

A penny dropped. Of course they were not fooled, realised the Chief Inspector! All over the world they roamed buying folk-songs, on their ten thousand bucks per year plus exes. There was not enough culture to go round: at least not to satisfy the post-mortem desires of Clarence J. Boddingham, and his wealthier rivals. All in it! Lawyers, collectors, Judges, God knew whom! The just-did-not-quite-make-it University Grade siphoned off into the foundations. After all, what was he himself doing for Sir Charles Fennel?

He smiled. "I congratulate you gentlemen for alighting upon such a fertile hoard."

"Wot did you say?" Old Mr Tubb was raring to fight.

"*Hoard*, you old fuel," said Mrs Tubb, "like what the Vicar is supposed to have under his mattress."

"Half of the collections for forty years." Tubb was lifted to another scent.

"Three and a half thousand," said the black American, writing it in on the memo of agreement.

"I'm being got at," said the old man. "For two pins I'd write to the *News of the World*."

Mr Bones gave a whine and Harry glimpsed Honeybody's leer—the Sergeant had cottoned on too.

"Perhaps you'll witness the signature, sir, as we like to make it impartial."

The Chief Inspector dragged out his ballpoint and obliged.

"And when can we have another?" wheedled Billy the Song and the old man bridled. "Sometimes I wake up scared. It's not the Devil, him being a civil man and a life peer, but the Imps!"

Charlotte Chuck gave him a glare, and he hurriedly signed on the remains of an old billiards table.

Harry and the dog preceded Honeybody back to the bar. "A racket by the old gents I saw this afternoon," he said. "He'd do the songs—the Professor I mean—and his brother would provide the know-how."

"They are all in it today," said Honeybody. "The wife's cousin used to make trousers, ruinin' her eyes for the eighteen bob making-up fee they pay out of Savile Row. So she started buying the cabbage—that's the bits of stuff they have left over—and cutting them out herself with a slightly twisted arse-piece. Then she got a barrow and sent her husband—a useless sort named Perce—out with it with a card 'Savile Row Rejects from Famous Maker ... £3.17.4d.' Last I heard she's got a loft with six girls and a second-hand Jag. They're all in it except us, and when you come to think of it what are we doing except fiddling with a bit of second-hand crime, eh?"

Honeybody was already, in his mysterious fashion, accepted—absorbed might be the better word—into the Grey Goat, but, less sociable by nature, Harry stood back and watched the huge man join a darts side, pleading Mr Bones' allergy to the game as his own excuse. To keep the dog away, he took his own pint in its pewter pot and went "out the back", that universal amalgam of old bottles and latrine smells outside the kitchen.

He paced slowly up and down, marvelling at Mr Bones' intent to christen every one of the many crates, including soft drinks. While the big dog performed incredible feats of incontinence, he enjoyed the softness of the night and the faint smell of steak-and-kidney which was gradually mastering that from the ancient back lavatories.

"It's like this," said a small breathless voice from behind. It was the girl, Charlotte.

"You will really have to finish your sentences when you work in Fleet Street," he said amused, while Mr Bones, who had some kind of fixation, caressed her ankles.

She laughed. "I did not know policemen were like you."

He kept silent.

"The uncles have no money you know and I haven't a penny. I mean nobody has ever been able to employ them for very long: not quite Establishment types although the Family is goodish in its way. Bull and the poor old Colonel ruined us. My father tried everything, but he had the good old anti-Midas touch. I scarcely remember him or my mother. Only John and Paul, the dearest things."

"I think *you* are a funny thing," said Harry, as she took his tankard and swigged.

"The Saxons did that when they liked anybody," she said. "Oh, I know hundreds of out-of-the-way things like that. All useless, and when Uncle John got me to ballet school through influence I was too big round the bottom. At least they were good enough to tell me, probably because I was not paying a fee, otherwise they'd have kept me stewing around. Tell me, you will introduce me in The Street?"

For a moment the Chief Inspector thought of that mythical area known as "The Street" which disconcertingly assumed a real life of its own when least expected. In fifteen years' time she would be broad-bottomed and immensely capable, perhaps talking of "her" page.

"I will," he said, "introduce you to the nastiest types who ever fudged an expense sheet with alacrity, plus a few of the

Greater, Pastmaster Beasts who watch them like hawks. I must tell you that I was thinking of giving you advice on the 'Be Good Sweet Maid' principle, but having observed your talent for larceny introduce you I shall."

In the light of the thirty-watt globe, swinging on its fraying piece of flex outside the coal shed, he thought he saw her pout.

"They can afford it," she said. "I thought it up a year ago when they first started coming here. Credulous, badgering the old soaks for songs and old caperings. All they knew is some of the dirty 'Coal Hole' songs of the nineteenth century and the 'Lambeth Walk'. So I approached the uncles. The bank was being very bitchy about the second mortgage, or maybe it was the third. It's funny, they are honourable men, Paul has got the D.S.O., but my, when the Establishment really gets its back to the wall it can fight. Or fiddle."

"That is precisely why it *is* the Establishment," the Chief Inspector told her.

"In any case the Americans have got so much money it drips out of their ears. It's all bra and corset money."

"I know," the Inspector sighed, deciding that moral homilies were out of place.

"For being nice, I've got something for you." She fumbled with the back of her tight pants.

"It" was a silver flask, the pigskin half-covering dull and greasy looking.

"The inscription is engraved on it," she said as Harry peered in the dim light. "It is just 'to my darling Ossie from Penelope'. It is a bit on the choking side."

"And where did you get it?"

"In the Inquest Room upstairs. That room really has the rubbish of years over all the little shelves. I could make a good few quid dealing in it, only the landlord is too cunning to sell. Anyway I was prying, looking for something small and valuable to pinch," she laughed, "and came across this. I would say you should pay me a fiver."

The Chief Inspector got his last one out of his wallet—Elizabeth having exacted double house-keeping because of it being a holiday—and exchanged it.

"I wonder how the devil it got there? It was not produced in evidence."

"Carelessness?" said the girl. "When it is over—I mean whatever you're doing—I shall write it up. I took a picture of it with Paul's great old plate camera he used on 'digs'."

"Somebody had it there ready, I suppose," said Harry, wrapping it in a handkerchief, "but decided not to call it into evidence. Though I wonder why the hell not: perhaps the news leaked out of the second flask."

"Are you thinking of fingerprints?" said the girl.

"A good sweaty print, and Penelope was eating a meal, will sort of engrave into silver if not cleaned pretty soon. This one looks as though it has been a hundred years without paste being put on it. She would have perhaps left an inky fingerprint somewhere in her diary: bound to in fact in those pre ballpoint days. A nice job for the local forensic boys, they love esoteric problems. Then we'll analyse the inside—antimony forms an opaque film on metal or glass, dissolvable in a weak acid solution."

"And you prove?"

"We establish that he was probably poisoned by antimony—the hospital reports of that day are always a bit suspect: there was a tendency not to clean the apparatus properly: further that he did get it out of the flask handled by Miss Penelope."

Enough was enough. She was too attractive to tête-à-tête with in the backyards of pubs.

IV

HE BREAKFASTED EARLY while the rest of the house was still abed, except for Amanda and Mr Bones, who shared the scrambled eggs and toast which he cooked for himself. The Chief Constable, Colonel Angel, was a non-sleeper who relieved his condition by being at his desk by seven and like most people with vices tended to favour those who shared them. It was half past seven when the Chief Inspector stopped the car outside the old-fashioned early Victorian police station, with its statue of Justice and clock with irremediably slow insides.

The Colonel was a big, deceptively slow man with steady grey eyes. He listened and without comment summoned a smart young technician whose eyes glistened as he wrapped the old diary and the flask in specially prepared sheets of paper. If it was there he'd get it, he assured them.

"He will at that," said the Chief as the door closed. "Lady Fennel is a romantic American—landing people on the Moon," he snorted, "and trying to help people who won't help themselves. If you establish the poison was in this flask and that Penelope's prints were on it you have a foolproof case for a jury."

"It does not quite clinch it," said Harry. "As she was the donor she had ample reason to have handled both flasks in her time. Besides, our Mr Hawker has a file on 'possible methods of death'."

"I'd hate to get on the wrong side of your Mr Hawker," laughed the Chief.

"We had a case wherein a whole family was poisoned. It was in a quart bottle of beer. It transpired that the bottle went back forty years and we thought it must have been in a garden shed"—the Chief Inspector gestured, making shapes with his hands—"full of broken pots, old tins, broken implements, filled originally with an antimonial garden solution. The liquid in which it was suspended evaporated, leaving the film. Now somebody turned it in for the deposit and bottling machinery cannot, or at least could not fifteen years ago, cope with arsenical or antimonial film. Beer or spirits gradually dissolves the film when the bottle is filled. It all leaves room for a fascinating criminal idea, with infinite variations."

"Nobody was a scientist around the case. Oh, I didn't know it," said the Chief Constable, "but old Charles Fennel came bustling round with a précis."

"I do not think that it would need a Pasteur to perhaps stumble on that one. Anybody keeping antimony in solution in a clear bottle could surely see the film form. But there was a scientific connexion. I was reading the great bundle of paper in bed"—he saw, slyly, the approval in the Chief's face: after all, there was nothing against making virtue out of necessity and the twins had conjointly wailed until three in the morning—"and there was some association between the officers of the Regiment and St Beedle's Hospital, a now defunct teaching hospital. Traditionally the Regimental Surgeons came from the hospital, there were a couple of annual functions—a river picnic and a cricket match. A kind of camaraderie grew up between the men, at any rate the younger men. You must remember that London hospitals in those days . . ." He left the sentence to stew in its own juice.

"Able to wander about at will over the hospital, you mean. The Victorians were fond of that pursuit, and God knows there was enough poison around. You fancy this Major Bull as the villain, of course."

"Bradstreet faced a kind of ruin," Harry shrugged, "but not an irrevocable one, although infinitely painful—no more cigars and braised pheasant unless tasting of charity. But Major Bull faced red ruin. Colonel taps at his room, leaves loaded pistol, hrmphs 'you know what to do, sir', and leaves. Oh, God, I forgot..."

"That I was a Colonel? Different generation, old son. *Beau Geste* and all that, eh? Y' know, I think that was a bit of exaggeration, London in those days being full of almost cashiered officers, 'resign or' types, you know. It is much simpler nowadays, just leave it to the accountancy branch to keep us all straight. Nevertheless it meant red ruin to Bull. You couldn't get a job as a tapster after court martial. It left card-sharping in France and Germany, blackmail or poncing if you had superior talent in an over-crowded market. Fencible Regiments were not quite 'the thing', you can see that from the social background. A foot guards officer would scarcely have given the time of day to an architect or physician, let alone a surgeon. I would judge both Bradstreet and Bull to be typical red-faced, over fed and drunk, middle-Victorian bores."

"I wonder why Bradstreet joined a fencible show: he does not seem to have been cowardly."

"Cowardly? The Victorians did not have the same views about serving abroad: you went if it coincided with your ethical or financial wishes. In the last war Canada still kept a 'home fires only' area of recruiting. In the States the National Guard only go abroad on declaration of war, and not at the whim of any politician who dislikes a regime. Hrmph. There I go. The Colonel Syndrome, but it clears the head mightily. A fencible, my dear sir, was a good, fashionable reason for existence in the days when trade was considered low."

Harry's watch read eight forty-five as the red telephone rang.

The Colonel's mottled hand took the handset up. He listened. Rattled, read Harry, but the unflappable type at bottom. "All right, carry on." The Chief Constable hung up.

"Good man, my Superintendent on murder, not that we have half a case a year, rest of the time he is on other duties. Gerald Snape found dead, knife through his heart, plumb centre, by the early morning cleaner in his office at Little Brittox, that's near the Cathedral. You saw him after our telephone conversation yesterday?"

"Half an hour. I thought he was all you said. A sly fellow on the cruel cat-and-mouse side."

"The body is cooling. The Super used a thermometer. I'd trust him more than the surgeon, a youngish fellow. Super says death was between nine and nine thirty last night."

"He narrows it," said Harry, perhaps a bit sourly.

"He spent fifteen years in D Division before he swapped down here. Knows his onions, or cadavers if you prefer."

"Weapon?"

"Cheap kitchen knife, mass-produced for fancy French cooks who read magazines. New, he thought, and therefore with a good edge. It being a stuffy old night he was in a white broadcloth shirt, of the old cricketing type but better than synthetic for drinking up the sweat, and St Michael slacks."

"I don't think he was the kind of man who wore informal clothes on formal occasions," grunted Harry. "A semi-off-record gathering, one thinks."

"That's a point." The Chief made a note. "As a fresh eye, though," he was warning Harry, "you might come and have a look-see. I'll give my Super an hour, not wishing to perform one's official tasks officiously, about the only talent needed for this particular job, y' know. Tell you what, can you abide breakfast at this hour?"

Harry shrewdly diagnosed a slight grog blossom on the Colonel's temple and said quickly: "As a drinker, sir, no, except anchovy toast."

"But that's what I have at nine o'clock here," said the Colonel with joy, "plus strong Java coffee to tone up the linings. Join me. The staff think I'm mad."

Harry drank coffee that made his hair stand on end and ate Gentleman's Relish on brown toasted bread. Absentmindedly he looked under the desk for his slippers.

"Snape did a bit in the money-lending," said the Colonel, wiping his mouth with a tissue.

"Above legal limit?"

"A good solicitor does not have legal limits. The Snapes have always lent money in a refined and expensive way. They ruined poor old Colonel Chuck when he was in difficulties—I heard that long before you told me the cause."

"Tell me about Snape, rid your mind of it, and I'll take a note for you."

"Pushing forty," said the Colonel, "but first things first. The first Snapes were sixteenth century, lay ecclesiastical attorneys around the cathedral close. You needed them in those days when the Bishop had a Court and could bedevil an honest man. Nobody of course ever really likes a solicitor. Counsel, big, soapy men, are different, charmers, or I must admit charming little men," the Chief had diplomatically observed the Chief Inspector's five feet eight, "but solicitors tend to be caddish, wife-swapping men, as I find."

"They have to be a leetle bit eccentric to balance their daily life," said the Chief Inspector, circumspectly, because you could not afford to offend solicitors, even though this one was dead.

"We'll see," said the Chief, pressing a button which in turn produced more coffee, "but he was the last of the Snapes, they having been here for three centuries. Up and down like all the old families, but hanging on well, from church matters to conveyancing and estate managing, broadening their outlook a hundred years ago to divorces and even criminal stuff if the money was right. They used to own land—younger sons—but the family gradually reduced itself to Gerald. Money? Difficult to say. He would be comfortably off. His father might have been rich but reputedly came a hell of a cropper in 1947 in mining shares. But money was no object from our standards. Gerry practised because the family always had. Women?" The Chief shrugged. "He lived here in an own-your-own flat, a biggish block with a heated bathing pool and a restaurant. I think a servant came in all day. He entertained well, but had the local catering firm in to do the necessary. Oh, women friends, but rather of the hard-driving, tolerant divorcee type. Somebody told me that he had decided to procreate and was looking round for a mate with suitable financial expectations, just bitchy gossip at the club. We were all a bit jealous of Gerald. Well-heeled, even keel, impeccable future unless he assaulted a client, a little pied-à-terre in London, a boat down at Folkestone, a hundred yards of good fishing rights thirty miles away. He was intelligent, well-read and that I thought him a little bastard is just an old man's prejudice. Hrmph."

"The money-lending business interests me. Comfortable bachelors who lend money in a shady way sometimes succumb to a shrewdly riven kitchen knife."

"We will probably find it so. The office safe was open—not the strong room in the basement which is first class, but the flimsy one in Snape's room. Stamp money, current business, that sort of thing, one imagines. There has always been this back-wash of Snapian gossip. Ill-disposed parties whispering behind their hands: 'He's seeing Snape!' And I suppose ninish at night—there is an alley at the side of the building with a kind of back door, lock and hinges oiled, reports my Super—is the sort of time one imagines money-lenders of the semi-legal kind may operate."

"He would do it through a third party, a Mr Brown, man of straw," sighed Harry who had experience of the trade. "I worked on the Squad for a bit. You virtually cannot get them. The Brown is really a twenty-five notes a week clerk, shrewd at figure work and clever enough to know nothing. The whole transaction is a legal fog, but enforceable by the money-lender. It is not an industry where there is any place for a fool-on the lender's side of the counter. On the other side," he shrugged.

"One is afraid that the late Snape will not be mourned," said he Colonel.

"And that will make your job that much more difficult," said Harry, leaning back.

The Superintendent (a first-class man, diagnosed Harry) was amiable to the Chief Constable, a little sniffy to the Chief Inspector. The late Snape was on a stretcher as they arrived, the black haft of the kitchen knife protruding from the dark, congealed blood on the white shirt front.

A pair of typists were tear-stained in the outer office.

"One of the partners is in," said the Super, "the other two who work here—they have four offices—being out on business." He looked at Snape's diary. "Nothing. The condition of the Firm is that Snape owned it: the partners were very much working partners. About the money-lending side, they preferred to know nowt. I gather from the managing clerk that anything which Snape did in this direction was very much his own pigeon. Oh, well, there are the photographers knocking off!"

"I do not like it very much," said the Chief Constable.

"It takes a bit of expertise to stab a person through his ticker," said Harry. "Most people would go too far to the left, eventually fatal, but causing a lot of interim unpleasantness."

"He knew the killer," said the Superintendent, "probably under-estimated him when he made his demands for money. The man produced the knife, did him, took the notes of hand and decamped. I would say a man of a certain scientific knowledge of anatomy."

"I could not quarrel with that," said Harry, "the inference being that Snape used to leave his side door open when engaged on money-lending. Did anybody see anything?"

"This part of the town is dead after eight o'clock," said the Chief. "The alleyway runs between these offices and the side wall of a deep lock-up shop. There was a police patrol at nine p.m., midnight, four a.m. and seven. That's all our resources run to, but there never has been anything here that I recall."

"A stolen cycle was abandoned here three years ago!" grunted the Super. "Even the shops aren't the kind to attract breaking, and there is a bank near by with a night safe."

"Mr James said the loans would ostensibly be made by a man of straw," said the Chief and the Superintendent grunted dolefully in agreement. "The easiest way is make the mark sign for five hundred and give him two hundred and fifty," he said. "I am very much afraid that we shall find that Snape's two hands knew nothing of each other's work. I do not want to be pessimistic, but crimes of this nature often remain unsolved by their very nature. Steps will be taken to sift all papers, business and private, check all his acquaintances and enquire of all local householders, such as they are."

Harry nodded. It was standard procedure.

"We'd better check his service flat," said the Chief Constable. "Care to come, Mr James?"

Reluctantly the Chief Inspector deferred to rank: in situations of this nature you got all the kicks and none of the ha'pence.

"I think," said the Chief Constable in the police car, "that you might hold down a very gentle watching brief, Mr James. One can see the headlines—'Well-known county solicitor slain near Cathedral'—and if the Super's forebodings are justified we will be dumping the baby in your people's laps in due course."

This time it was Harry's turn to grunt.

Snape had lived in what was the country by today's standards, opposite a carefully preserved village green with a suitably green and slimy pond and the old parish pump. There were four lifts, three of them self-operated, the fourth manipulated by a man in a splendid uniform. Eventually they found the Manager, who knew the Colonel.

"Terrible business," he said after explanation, "I understand he was the last of an old family. Quiet man, didn't see much of him, paid by banker's draft." He looked at his watch. "We'd better go up in the lift, the daily woman comes in from ten thirty until four. He would have the place shined and polished very thoroughly. A Mrs Beckett, been here for some years, cleans the lifts out at five thirty, then home to breakfast, here again at nine to mop the foyer, then on to Mr Snape."

They went through the anonymous door. The floors were tiled and a diminutive woman was washing them.

"I am afraid that Mr Snape died at his office."

"The bed was not slept in: I was wondering what I should do," she said matter-of-factly, wiping her hands on her apron.

"Just continue. We'll look around."

It had two bedrooms, two living-rooms and was quietly luxurious. The impression was of comfort, but in a spick and span way with a dustpan never too far away. Harry raised his eyebrows at the number of suits in the built-in closet.

Something was wrong. The furniture was too modern. He said so.

"The old family house where he lived with the parents went up, holus-bolus, in 'forty-four. He was a child. Gerald's tastes ran to modernity," said the Chief Constable, his eyes missing nothing. Harry sighed as he saw the lines of bookshelves, each volume requiring scrutiny. Fortunately there were no files, Gerald Snape evidently not bringing work home. In one room was a desk, drawers empty, no typewriter. There was a green blotting pad. Snape had been a doodler of concentric circles. In large writing was the word "Collingwood".

The Superintendent made a note. "Can't recall anybody of that name."

Mrs Beckett had no feeling for Mr Snape because she had rarely seen him, being out of the house when he returned and being paid by the Manager. She did not work Sundays, when Mr Snape adequately cared for himself.

"A better cook than most gentlemen, judging from the washing-up," she said in her gasping little voice.

"Did women stay here?" asked the Super.

"I never saw no sign."

Chief Inspector James left the two older men to it and went down to the garage area. A man was hosing cars.

"Mr Snape's, sir? The Bentley over there. I only clean it once a week as he only uses it week-ends. There is an excellent bus service into town and parking's a nightmare today."

A discreet man, Mr Snape, preferring the anonymity of a bus to the advertisement of a Bentley, thought Harry as he followed suit. Out of curiosity he got out and walked to Snape's office. There was a small crowd on the footpath. A vast man with a camera looked at Harry speculatively. With him was the girl, Charlotte, clutching a notebook. Recognition dawned on the man's face and the camera swung upwards.

It rarely did much good to try to dodge except that the resultant print made you look ridiculous.

"Use your eyes, girl," rumbled the man. "It's Inspector James of the Yard. He's a homicide specialist."

"Terry", that was the man's name, but whether it was his Christian or surname Harry was unsure.

"Fact is, Terry, I came down on Sunday on holiday with the wife."

"He's been looking up an old murder," said Charlotte. "Up to something."

"What about a drink?" said Terry. He already smelled of sherry and the Chief Inspector remembered hearing that he had drunk himself out of Fleet Street.

There was an old pub under the very gables of the Cathedral. The Inspector bought a double sherry, staring meaningfully at the Australian bottle, and two light shandies.

"The P.R.O. said he was stabbed," said the photographer, "with a kitchen knife."

"That is correct."

"Well, thank God for small mercies. Ferrety little man, weren't he?"

"I cannot be quoted."

"Right."

"Then I think he was. He lived luxuriously, but very secretively, seeing clients in the evenings apparently."

"Now, poppet," said Terry, "any journalist worthy of his beer can spin that out to three hundred ill-chosen words. 'Dead man's Secrecy and Luxury, say Locals.' If we don't make a tenner each on linage you can call me mud." He swilled half the sherry and lowered his voice.

"What about his woman?"

The Inspector kept silent, often the most skilled form of lying.

"I'd go along, but she wouldn't give the time of day, but if I had a rozzer, even one on holiday, with me it might work."

Harry thought that if he took the gross man to police headquarters he would merely plead Press privilege, a mythical condition but one which nobody in public life much wanted to contest.

"As long as you get it straight that I am on holiday, doing a private job of a literary nature."

"It's sixty miles away," said Terry. "We need a car, mine being under repair."

"They repossessed it," said Charlotte, but her colleague took no umbrage. "That's the spirit, luv, that's what gets you a byline. Cheek and taking dead liberties."

"Can I hire one?" Elizabeth did not expect him home, and it would be quicker. Almost inevitably the gross man knew where and after one more round and some telephoning they were driving north-east, towards the Bristol Channel, Harry preferring to take the wheel.

Like most of his profession, Terry could not remain more than half n hour in utter silence.

"One of the flukes," he said. "Damn me, you start to realise how the blackmailers get their grist. A year ago I was in London in a Lyons Tea Shop, eyes closed, they know me there. Between you and me I'd had a little skinful. But, y'know, I get to the stage where I can hear and remember it clear next day, a rare faculty. I heard two voices, a deep woman's and a light-tenored man's. They had obviously dismissed me as a piece of wood. Anyway, they were not talking loud—the place was about filled, everybody minding their own little business at four in the arvo. People who've come off shift, shoppers going home, you know. They were a pair of crooks, my dear sir. The talk was of lending large sums at illegal interest, taking part in crooked transactions, and fiddling stock-exchange regulations. He was ticking her off. Nasty little cutting-edged voice he had. He was in fact telling her to mind her side of the business and leave the brainwork to himself. I took a look. Now this was not really a coincidence, but something that can happen any day. Fifteen years ago I attended the funeral of a Lady Cynthia Lambone Pye. I'm fond of odd things and looked up *Burke's Peerage*. A Barony created in seventeen summit, believed to be traced from the Conqueror's henchman, one Le Bon Pied. I got another book and exposé on such things, and the progenitor was a pie-maker who came from the village of Lambourne in 1690 and fairly cleaned up, his son marrying well. But I remembered the face of one of the Lambone Pyes, fifteen years old lady, a laughing girl with a long nose transformed into a thirty-year-old woman who was not laughing. There was no laughter in the voice either.

"It didn't matter to me one bit, there's no point in trying to follow up a story of this nature: anyhow nobody's interested and you might wait years for the informer's fee the Inland Revenue pay.

"But then, six weeks ago I came to Greymouth and there was the other bit in the jigsaw, Mr Gerald Snape. Again, no interest, not being in the blackmailing line, and I would have guessed Mr Snape a slippery customer to screw down. Her name, by the way, is Lady Joanna Pye." With the air of a man who has delivered everything the photographer fell comfortably asleep.

"What shall we say to her?" whispered Charlotte.

"I'll think of something." Five miles on and thirty from Greymouth he prodded Terry awake, the man switching on immediately. "I made a detour a few weeks ago coming back from the Assizes and remember it well."

"It" was a delightful Queen-Anne cameo, perhaps a large dower house in its day. Harry stopped outside the porticoed front door.

An old parlour maid doubtfully stated that my lady was in. Now the Inspector became conscious that he himself was in holiday attire, that Terry's suit was vast, baggy, patched on one rump and liberally anointed with stains of assorted description, while the zip on Charlotte's pants had jammed so that brown skin showed through.

He took out his professional card and scribbled: "Re Gerald Snape deceased." If that did not catch the trout, nothing would.

They waited twenty minutes, doubtless, thought the Inspector, while Lady Joanna prudently telephoned the Snape office. He examined old portraits, noted that the house was in impeccable repair, but that it was not quite original as to furnishing, as though old pieces had been sold in bad times but recently replaced.

"Come this way." The maid was disapproving.

Lady Joanna inhabited a large sunlit room pleasantly but austerely furnished. She did not rise from behind the big desk. Somewhere there was the noise of a typewriter.

She had once been darkly lovely, could have been now if the mouth had not been compressed into a thin slit, while the lines of avarice stretched down from the nose to the corners of her cheeks. Her figure was slim—too much so—but in its way perfect. She was dressed in a simple (Harry guessed terribly expensive) suit.

"I understand, Inspector, from his subordinates that Gerald Snape was murdered. You will permit me to say that this does not appear to be what one has expected from a police visit. I am a reader," she gave a wintery smile, "of Agatha Christie."

"You must forgive me, Lady Joanna, for not being pear-shaped, moustachioed and with curious English. I am a Scotland Yard Chief Inspector down at Greymouth to do some research for Sir Charles Fennel. By permission of the local authorities I have a vague watching brief in the case of Mr Snape. My companions are two local journalists. They told me they intended to interview you, so, well, I came along informally with the object of saving you embarrassment."

The violet eyes were momentarily approving, but her voice was dry. "My father spent some years in the Foreign Office, Inspector, persuading unfortunate natives that it was good for them. You may as well be seated."

The chairs were hard: the kind of chair that predatory business men fa. , a pain in the back making it much easier for the client to agree to extortion. Harry ostentatiously sat on the extreme edge of his. He saw, from his eyes' corners, that Charlotte had cocked her right leg in a ballet pose. Only poor Terry, imprisoned by weight and alcohol, looked like a frightened cow.

"I have heard it alleged that you were involved in business transactions, your ladyship, with the late Mr Snape. You will appreciate that we have to 'draw a portrait' of deceased in a murder case. Any scrap of information is of value, and thus I merely ask you for such comments as good citizenship might impel."

"And the Press?"

"The law of libel, the Press Council plus our innate good taste protects you," said Charlotte, wiggling her foot.

"You are the Chunk girl who was too heavy *derrière* for the ballet," said Lady Joanna without emotion. "My family and yours were acquainted. I must say I am glad to see a spark of spirit animating what were a soft lot. My own circumstances, though more exalted socially, were similar. You may call here at any time you are passing. And I see that the stout gentleman has photographic gear attached to his naval and I eat photographers before breakfast."

A slim hand took a cigarette from its box and snapped the lighter while Harry was half-way to his feet.

"I was the front end of a financial car that Snape drove," she said. "When the only other true Lambone Pye died, an old aunt, Snape was the executor. He suggested that I should act as, say, Managing Director to his Chairman. I was penniless: this house was third mortgaged. Snape in the course of his work often knew of business opportunities which he could not exploit because of his position."

"Of trust?"

"I know nothing of it. He was the lawyer and vetted the legal end. I found I had some slight talent for business. The Estate is now disencumbered of debt. The Lambone Pyes have not been driven out by the Welfare State."

There was a touch, more than a touch, of passion. Of course! Megalomaniac on the subject of Family and

Possessions, thought Harry. But was not this megalomaniac outlook the very fibre of so much of history, the motivation of centuries, perhaps the key to Western civilisation? He decided to say nothing.

"I have no knowledge of anyone who might have had reason to kill Snape. One imagines that people are not killed in the way of business."

"I noticed that you have a system of alarms on doors and windows."

This time her laugh was genuine. "Oh, I'm a collector in my acquisitive way. One must say that lawyers are more to be feared than assassins."

"What were your feelings towards Mr Snape? Pray do not answer if you find this an impertinence."

"I would not. Oh, Snape was useful: a dominating rather snobbish little man. He descended from ecclesiastical lawyers and blood has the unfortunate habit of outing." Her face was momentarily very proud. "I went along with him because I am damned if we—I have a very distant cousin, aged thirteen—are going to be thrown in Mr Wilson's dustbin."

Three years ago the Chief Inspector had had a painful growth on one foot removed at no cost by the Welfare State* and he now felt a twinge of guilt as he caught Lady Joanna's eye. He should have paid the twenty guineas required to have it excised privately, perhaps saving the last taxational straw laid upon some stately house! One felt like a tumbrel taking the Lady Joannas of life to extinction or prostitution and all for free cough mixture: not even from political passion or desire for revenge.

"Now, your ladyship," Terry was on his feet, "I'll be frank. I can get a photo syndicated which means maybe fifty

* See *Death and Mr Prettyman*

quid, as an exclusive. But I have to have a bit of guff for a longish caption. Your ancestry is in the various books, but for the 'live' interest can I say, 'Glamorous Lady Joanna, long-time friend of Gerald Snape, describes him as gentle, intellectual and strangely fascinating'?"

"Oh, God!" She laughed again, an iceberg partly thawed. "A Snape! I'm sorry to sound Dickensian. But a Snape! But, well, if you badger me no more you can use it."

"Look as though you were pleasant but a mite solemn." Terry balanced his Linhof on top of his stomach and took three rapid shots, while Lady Joanna consciously relaxed the planes of her face.

"About only the second sensational murder around Grey-mouth," said Chief Inspector James, slyly.

Lady Joanna's face, momentarily so much younger, had closed like a sliding door.

"You mean Penelope Fennel? She was rather a pet of my great-grandfather. He was Lord Lieutenant of the County and what interest he could exert he did. The Fennels, nice parvenus then as now, were protégés of my family. Now, of course," she grimaced, "they have grown gilt wings of their own. Snape's ancestor did the brief for Penelope at the Inquest, a scandalous affair by all accounts. It was strange that Gerald should have suddenly, some months ago, developed such an abiding interest in the old Fennels. Old family albums that are still in our archives, with those wooden photographs and before that the little water colours, so much better."

Terry bridled, thought to defend his craft, subsided with a soft belch.

"I may as well tell you," said Harry, "that Sir Charles wishes to have published a re-examination of the case against his great-aunt, which seems on evidence to be flimsy."

"I suppose Gerald was buttering up Fennel," she said. "He was not above it, tongue in cheek. I asked him once, and he said there was no doubt she did it. He was above her in station, you know."

With this *non sequitur* in his mind, Harry expressed thanks, congratulated himself upon proficient thin-ice skating, and led his flock back to the car and thence to the cheap pull-up for carmen known to Terry where they had excellent shepherd's pie and afterwards an illicit quart of beer.

V

HAVING MADE HIS report—typed to avoid possibly troublesome nuances of human relationships—to the Chief Constable, the Chief Inspector luxuriated at ease for eight days, compiling fifteen thousand words *in re* Captain Oswald Bradstreet deceased, not that he was so pompous but he rather thought that Sir Charles Fennel might favour this kind of approach, with little bits of dog Latin: Chairmen did. Mr Bones, overcome by the heat and favours of the bitch owned by the gate-keeper, lay peaceably all day in a ring of slobber: the twins were similarly stertorous and Amanda developed a technique, not too painful, of biting his knee while he pecked out his type-written draft, Honeybody, smelling of Cologne, feeding him with rough notes.

Two days after Snape's death a long memorandum came from the local forensic lab. Boiled down, it said: "The diary contains three well-marked prints of what is almost certainly a right index finger, one in the ossified remainder of what was probably a cosmetic cream, the other two in black ink of the kind used in the diary and a common formula in those days. On the silver flask, there is—among twenty others—a similar print etched from oils used in the making of brandy. There is around eighty per cent probability of it being from the same finger, but time has eroded the print. As far as the flask is concerned, it certainly contained antimony in the form of tartar emetic in massive quantity. The residual amount would possibly produce death within a few days."

Today, on a Wednesday, the War Office was dispatching

a full Colonel to see Harry as the result of enquiries he had "pursued" via a groaning Superintendent Hawker. This visitation was due at eleven a.m. and at the moment he was grooming a rather awed wife about entertaining War Office colonels.

"After all, they are the last line, aren't they?" Elizabeth was saying. "I mean when the politicos have made the final mess, they promote all the colonels to generals, like they did Eisenhower, and our destiny is in their hands. Do they like dry sherry?"

"Lightly refrigerated," insisted Harry, "ice-cold reminding them of morgues. But the biscuits must be on the sweetish side, like the conversation. And he must be banished by noon, for I have arranged for him to nosh with Lady Fennel."

By various female strategems the favourite frocks had arrived by parcel, and Elizabeth had been "taken up" by Lady Fennel to the extent of revising her previous poor opinion of Americans.

She could not present her colonel in the flesh, as the unofficial strivings of the Yard had unearthed a veritable Bradstreet, untitled, the baronetcy having succumbed, but living in Tooting and very willing to come to lunch and accept fifty guineas for the précis of family papers. Harry was dubious: one's ancestry—he had little, for himself, except a lady novelist of dubious virtue—was hardly a thing to flog for fifty guineas, but there you were in these unenlightened days.

The Colonel proved a nice mousy man with a liking for minor eighteenth-century poets: probably as a subaltern he quoted at Dunkirk, accurately.

"We would not want anything written about Colonel John Bull," he said, liking the slightly cool dry sherry and sweetish biscuits while his driver was regaled in the kitchen with cooler bottled beer by Honeybody.

"He took the money," said Harry, "and I do not think that unless you can persuade Sir Charles, or his good lady, you can stop it appearing in print."

"My masters hate print unless they are on the bellowing end of the tube." Like most of his kind he was intelligent and disconcertingly well educated.

"Stop it how?"

"Defence of the Realm Act."

"Sir Charles is an old Mother-of-Parliament hand who draws a lot of water. And what scandal really, compared with what you gents have got locked up?"

"I think I should have another. Do you fellows not have horrid secrets? I mean, who was Jack the Ripper?"

"Look in your files. But no doubt that Bull was embezzling?"

"None. In debt and poodle-faking. Captain Bradstreet was the auditor. Oh God, as much an auditor as my young daughter is a bookbinder. 'Sign here, please' and 'Yes, old man'."

"A good motive for murder."

"Apart from Territorials, Army officers murder—in peacetime, your wife is thinking from her Left-Wing look—remarkably few people. I have digested the statistics and we are indeed law-abiding beasts. And poison! A trained hand like Bull would surely have gone for an accident."

"Difficult to get into his mind," said the Chief Inspector. "Well, Colonel, I'll leave it to you and Sir Charles. I think we should publish."

He and Elizabeth had time for a quick dry sherry before the next visitor, the last survivor of the Bradstreet family, whom a hundred years of genealogy had transformed into a red-faced man named Headstone who smelled of stale sweat, wore a blue striped suit and travelled in something vague. Sir Charles had produced him via an advertisement in the *News of the World* and after a first swift glance Harry substituted beer for his "Dalucia" sherry and whispered to his wife to keep the meal down to soup, chops and a bit of inferior cheese. Sergeant Honeybody, reading the symptoms, was discussing ladies' underwear with Headstone, who was nursing a badly wrapped brown-paper parcel.

"You'll find everything all present and correct, Chief," the man said in mock public-school tones. "Let me see, the original patents of the baronetcy: the diary of the third holder of the title, an assorted handful of deeds and letters from attorneys, and the day book of poor old Oswald who bought it in 1874, covering 1870 to his death. Fair enough?"

The Chief Inspector passed over Sir Charles' cheque. Lunch was a miserable meal. Headstone talked only of mythical family fortunes taken away by evil doers and the Labour Party. Of Bradstreet he knew little except that he was "a guards officer who was murdered by a woman he had—pardon my French—got into the family way".

Apart from Honeybody the imperturbable and Amanda—who was developing a liking for low types—they were all glad to see the back of Headstone.

"It's almost frightening to see how these old families can decay. Less than a hundred years and from an official at Court to such a creature," decided Elizabeth. "The Fennels—or even ourselves—could do the same. It's frightening." She stretched out to touch Amanda.

"More likely the twins will start the toboggan," said Harry, piercing the crown of a cigar, "young women tending to marry a bit above themselves. But, you know, Headstone is the spitting image taking off twenty years of age, of Sir Ferguson Bradstreet, official at Victoria's Court. *Sartor Resartus* and all that. You often find this strong family likeness. . . ." The telephone rang.

It was Superintendent Hawker.

"How is it going, laddie?" His voice was suspiciously cajoling.

"Cannot grumble, Mr Hawker."

"But now you are going to. Chief Constable Angel has asked us to move in. He rather suggested you, but apart from that we have got such a sickness list that your name came up yesterday to be asked to come in on emergency."

Blackmailing old swine. The Chief Inspector waved down his wife's protest. She had the knack of hearing telephone calls from afar. He said: "Rank and pay from the first of this month."

"I shall be massacred for it," Hawker growned, "but yes, you blackmailing dog."

"Pot."

"What's that?"

"Me black kettle, very clean. I'll do me best, dear sir, sir. Elizabeth sends her disgust."

"Why?" said Elizabeth, spluttering.

"Now, my dear, let Father handle this his own way and we may be a few bob up in the bank."

"Have you got something up your sleeve?"

"A little rustling, merely like a dry snake. But as my step-up pay goes back to the first of the month, plus expenses—at any rate normal hotel ones—plus the fact that with unlimited supplies of beer and midnight oil and your assistance in the typing, I can fudge the necessary twenty thousand words, most of 'em done, for Sir Charles, we are likely to wax rich or at any rate out of hock."

"I'll start the finish of the typing to date as soon as I've washed the dishes and fed the twins."

"Sergeant, you are on double pay, and to hell with Whitehall."

"The fishing's been that bad—coarse, they call it, but it wouldn't be allowed in a self-respecting strip show—that double time, which means two-and-a-half after midnight, would by no means come amiss."

Making a firm mental resolve to let the wealthy Sergeant, waxing well as he knew upon the homping of fish and chips in south-east London, pay for all his own beer, the Chief Inspector telephoned the Chief Constable, announcing his confirmed rank for the first time with aplomb, and fixing an appointment.

"The fact is," said Colonel Angel, joviality vanished, in his office, "that nobody apparently could have killed Snape. He had four appointments in the afternoon, a Jones, a Fotherington, Ralf Fennel, and a Blairs, each about conveyancing small properties, two of them—Jones and Blairs—being estate agents. Snape was his usual coldly efficient little self. His notes are on his scratch pad in his impeccable, copy-plate writing. It was a busy day at the office, the two other resident partners working until eight. They dined together and provide a mutual alibi. The staff had gone at six. The partners poked their heads round the door of Snape's office and he said that he was getting up some county-court briefings—which was true—and might be around until ten. He had changed into slacks. The late Gerald, being unmarried, always liked to rub it in that he worked back several nights each week. You always find a fellow like that in the office making a virtue out of necessity," said the Chief, forgetting his own insomnia.

"But here enters a certain Mr James Cold, misnamed, and a Miss Jane, mini-skirted Smithers, a little trollop if I ever saw one but without any kind of a record. Aged twenty-two and eighteen respectively. In my young day..."

"My dear Colonel," said Harry.

"Oh, well, at least I used to have an old car. I suppose the credit squeeze has changed all that. As the evidence indicates, Snape used to open the side door into the alley. More people know Tom Fool than Tom Fool knows, one being Mr James Cold, a sharp, red-nosed lecherous little bugger one can say in honest appraisal, a clerk in the local Town Hall who has one hobby, the deflowering of young maidens, which he pursues with the utmost pertinacity."

A certain prostrate trouble, diagnosed Harry, such as can arouse old gentlemen to excessive censure.

"He knows every hay-loft, disused air-raid shelter, uninhabited alley, unfrequented doorway, and flight of back stairs in Greymouth. My night patrols constantly meet him buttoning up his fly. Hrmph. Anyway this weasel spotted the open door down the alley leading into Snape's office. Inside the hallway is a large closet, relic of some Victorian storage problem, with old furniture covers, files, and very comfortable for Mr James Cold it was.

"At eight thirty, after regaling Miss Jane Smithers with two gins and a portion of fried fish, Mr Cold lured her into this cupboard or closet and—is it wreaked or wrought for God's sake?"

"I think it is wreaked, sir," said Harry.

"Wrought," said Colonel Angel testily, "his horrid will, so the girl told me in tears, the hussy. If ever I saw a young lady who has been wreaked or wrought it is she. But they were there until ten thirty."

"Surely, in the circumstances love can be deaf as well as blind," suggested the Chief Inspector, "I mean among all those dusty Victorian files, somebody versus another body..."

"That lad has escaped horse-whipping and divorce actions too long to be discounted," said Colonel Angel. "His head, supported by Regina versus Samuel Lushington, if you please, a case tried in 1896 and now smeared with cheap brilliantine, was adjacent to the door, which he had left open two inches. I asked him what he would have done if the girl's two burly brothers had entered—not that they care for their womenfolk these days," he sighed, "—and the little swine said the technique was not to linger but to make a sudden, precipitous bolt for it, which always works if you are fast enough. As for the girl, between tears, leers and shy giggles, she said she heard nothing until she adjusted her clothing around ten fifteen. I tell you, Chief Inspector, the Superintendent here put them through the most minute cross-examination."

"When is the Inquest?"

"Tomorrow. We cannot hold up the Coroner any more. I may as well tell you that I am getting several sorts of hell. Snape was the possible Conservative candidate come next election, the present bloke considering retirement, and this plus influential friends around Whitehall results in half a dozen whining phone calls per day, each getting higher in rank. I sit here sweating that the Big Fellow himself will spare his gaze from higher things like Gibraltar and zero in on Greymouth."

"Fair enough," said Harry, "and you will call Miss Smithers and her, what is our term, oh yes, paramour, at the Inquest?"

"I have fee'd counsel to give them hell."

"In that case I shall ask to be quit of the case," said Harry firmly.

"Eh?"

"I shall inevitably, it seems, take the can back. Unsolved violence, probably a random crime. I do not want the additional publicity of having had two young people grilled for fornication, not for moral reasons or permissiveness—as a married man one is against fornication quite firmly—but because I do not want the murderer, whose identity I somewhat suspect, to know what these two did hear. I want them in this office pronto."

"Who do you suspect?" The Super was staring in disbelief.

"Superintendent, I felt a little tug on the line which could well make me look a complete and utter bloody fool and in practice seconded to the War Office. I will spare you and Chief any tar from my brush."

"Fair enough," said Colonel Angel at length.

"I do not know about married men being against fornication," said Sergeant Honeybody. "But deceased was not married. I've known money-lenders to take interest in kind. A dapper little fellow, was he not? Did women like him?"

"My wife said they detested him," said the Colonel. "Damp hands and smart innuendo. The ladies like a different technique these days, y' know: in temperament he was Edwardian or the twenties, too smart altogether."

"I should call his partner, Lady Joanna, or preferably get her in here by the threat of it."

"Shall be done. Oldish county family, the Lambone Pyes.

Prefer you to be careful. Oh, God, the things you have to take into consideration."

"Now," said Harry, "could he possibly have killed himself?"

"No fingerprints upon the knife, a Marks and Spencer job sold by the thousand. That does not necessarily mean gloves, as you know. A dry hand is liable not to leave prints. But my lads say that to sit down coldly at a desk and stab yourself like that is extremely unlikely. Your hand would fall off the knife most likely, but in the absence of a fare-ye-well note I and the Super crossed it off within a few hours. No evidence of dope, by the way, just the remains of the cold pork with salad and trifle he lunched off at the King's Hotel. He ate with a couple of barristers down here for the Assizes. The conversation was 'light' shop. He was not liked, by the by, but it is a fortunate barrister who does not lunch with a solicitor in the way of business. But both gentlemen were quite adamant that nothing possibly bearing upon murder was discussed. The transcript is here." He tapped a large file.

"The staff," asked Harry. "No evidence that they did it?"

"The other resident partners, who dined together, as was their custom once a week, alibi each other. The remaining staff, two male clerks, both elderly, and three women clerical workers, left the building at six. The senior clerk unsnibbed the lock of the front door and closed it. Keys are carried by him and by the partners. The back door on the alley was simply not used, except by Snape, who had an old key to the mortice lock. Apart from conspiracy—and the chartered accountant says the trust funds are in impeccable condition—I cannot see the motive."

"Could Snape have been trying to kick out one of the partners?"

"We checked that out. They were more or less employees,

but Snape paid very well: there is no smell of dislike or controversy in that quarter. He was not hail-well-met and the partners did not see him after six p.m. Consensus was that he was a cold, courteous fellow, highly efficient, who did not muzzle the local oxen. He was fond of money, but not to the point of petty economy, so it seems. I am told the staff were of high calibre and that Snape paid as well as anybody in the business."

"Heirs?"

"None whatsoever. And like many lawyers he did not leave a will. It looks as though he will have left a matter of ninety thousand in securities, plus the ninety per cent share of the business, which is problematical of course. The remaining partners told me they will try to buy it, though Snape *was* rather the business. In trouble you saw him first and he handed you over to a partner. No, the Government gets the lot, curse them."

"We civil servants cannot complain, sir," said Harry. "Look at it in the light that the efforts of the Snapes over the centuries will support a moderate-sized police force for a year. However the alternative is that somebody got into the office, concealed themselves, murdered Snape when all was quiet, and either went out by the front door at leisure, or used the door to the alley after ten thirty o'clock. The first question is whether anybody could get in unseen."

"It crossed my mind," said the Chief Constable, "but there seems a total absence of motive, except that Snape was screwing people for money. The lender was always Lady Joanna Lambone Pye, or a company of straw which she owned. She signed everything. Snape drew up the contracts: impeccable ones, but . . . A roguish business, our advisers say, which is why he used her as a front. There were records in his safe going back ten years. Some bad debts, but the mugs were shrewdly chosen and we think he made ten thousand a year from money-lending, tax free, as against six thousand, fully taxed, from his practice. He lived well, and there must have been a woman or women who cost a fair bit to keep. I suppose Lady Joanna might have got three thousand per year from the arrangement, enough to keep the ancestral home out of hock, which is her obsession. I suppose she'll carry on minus Snape and eventually trap herself. I questioned her and she just looked blank. As I said the Lambone Pyes are a very old family as things go."

The Chief Inspector remembered that the Colonel came of a very old, if rather proudly untitled, family indeed. As for looking blank, Harry had interviewed members of the peerage suspected of making their money in very strange ways and when questioned they always pulled a singularly blank expression out of the repertoire. But an ambitious policeman had to live with such things and he cleared his throat with suitable vassalage. "We'll treat the lady with great respect, sir. After all, it will eventually be a matter for the Inspection of Money-lenders' Branch. Fined eight hundred quid and let off to do it again. A lovely fiddle."

From the corner Honeybody boomed, "A curious thing, but if you ever arrest a money-lender you find a decayed gentleman, their last refuge so to speak. You often hear the Jews blamed, but it is usually the English aristocracy at it as they have been for these hundreds of years, begging your pardon, sir."

The Chief Constable was bellowing sneezes into a red handkerchief.

"This bloody hay fever," he said, without much conviction.

"None of the clients that came into that office on the day in question are under suspicion," said the Super, "because they returned to homes or offices and I think there is no probability of them retracing their steps to the office. There were four delivery boys, all accounted for. So that ruddy well leaves us with nobody."

But the Chief Inspector had opened the file and had spread out a large survey plan.

"The place seems full of old closets and unused rooms, Chief."

"It's a little gem of eighteenth-century architecture, but badly sited," mourned Colonel Angel. "As you say there were a dozen places for concealment, though you would have to know the building—that's a point."

"Barring collusion on the part of the staff, somebody must have got in: either they had a key to that front door or else Mr James Cold's pointed ears are not as efficient as he likes to think."

"I don't like the idea of the front door, the street is well lighted and the locks were changed only two years ago," said the Super.

"Oh well, the Sergeant and I will contribute what we can," said Harry diplomatically.

VI

It was one o'clock the next day that the Chief Inspector had one Mr James Cold and Miss Jane Smithers ushered into the rather charming, large early Victorian office that was lent him. He did this to avoid the gossip, scandalous charges perhaps of police officiousness, which would have resulted from their being summoned during working hours. Cold, who had reddish hair and a certain foxy, dapper charm, worked as a clerk at the Town Hall: his girl friend, with signs of incipient stoutness, was a friendly creature who worked in a shop purveying hand-made chocolates and marzipan.

"I'll keep it short," said Harry, "because you both made long statements a couple of days ago. What I want to know is are you certain of the time?"

"Positive, sir," said Cold, "my watch is a good one, a twenty-first present. We both had to get the last bus at eleven ten, so I had my eye on the time."

"And nobody walked past that cupboard while you were in it? One hard think please. Did you hear footsteps or any odd noises?"

"My attention was as it were divided," said Mr Cold, "and the two divisions I am sure about, but as to a third, well no, I could not express an honest opinion about odd noises."

"Miss, uh, Smithers?"

"I couldn't say, Chief Inspector, I'm sure, what with being very occupied as you might say, my boy friend having so many hands so it seems."

She was very pert and Harry gave an admonitory scowl. "The Inquest is held tomorrow." He cleared his throat.

"We bein' called?" There was a little whining alarm in Cold's voice.

"Your mum won't like it?" Harry addressed the girl, but she merely looked calculating, wondering, thought the Chief Inspector, exactly how she might cash in on the publicity, perhaps if public opinion might force Cold to do the "decent thing".

"Mrs Mayor won't like it," muttered Cold.

"That old moo isn't going to get it," said Miss Smithers enjoying herself.

"Now, Jane," said Cold, a touch of steel in his voice, "our dad went to a lot of crawling round getting me this fully pensionable job and prospects of being a municipal rent collector. I'd get kicked out of it if I did moral turpitude."

"What's that? We never got round to it." Jane giggled.

"That's enough out of you babies," said Harry James. "I won't call you to the Inquest. But you clear off and keep your little traps shut or I will call you in front of the Lady Mayor, who is a Magistrate. Trespass, indecent exposure, fornicating to the public nuisance, in fact half a dozen charges, all carrying a fortnight inside, twenty pounds and costs."

In this day and age people, particularly young people, were always conscious of the powers of officialdom which could often make life excessively unpleasant, and even Jane Smithers' buoyancy had dropped several degrees as they went out. Harry was much inclined to accept Cold's story as fact, but he would be a bad witness because of his habit, probably ingrown, of using too many words, product of incessantly talking to young women.

Now to see the four callers Snape had had in the afternoon. He supposed they would have to repeat the process with all morning callers at the office, who seemed to have numbered around fourteen.

Honeybody ushered them in one by one.

Charles Fotherington, living in a boarding house, came from Barrow-in-Furness. He was buying a row house because he was getting married. Occupation, panel-beater, aged forty-two. He had heard of Snape in a public house, phoned him up and went to see him about conveyancing and a possible mortgage. Snape's firm had clients who invested in property mortgages. He had never seen Snape before. He had paid forty-five pounds by cheque and was worried about it.

Harry reassured him. He had left Snape at three p.m. and having taken an afternoon off went straight home and had a celebratory glass of sherry with his landlady, a woman of impeccable character. Nevertheless Harry dictated a telex to Barrow-in-Furness. Check on one Charles Fotherington. Any connexion with a man named Gerald Snape, descriptions follows." More work for the constabulary's feet.

Charles Jones, a caller at three, was an estate agent. Snape did his legal work and had for years. "What a loss he will be for sure, as sharp a man as you could get on your side." At three thirty he decided to call it a day and went home to his wife and two young children under five.

"This is a terrible thing, Chief Inspector," said Ralf Fennel scrubbing his dark face with a red handkerchief. He was a man who sweated profusely.

"Damned hot," said Harry, amiably calling for two cups of coffee.

"Where we farmed at Grafton," said Ralf, "a hundred with humidity was nothing, but I never felt the heat. Likewise in the Desert. Many blokes used to just dehydrate, but never me."

Harry pushed forward the cigarette box. "What time did you see Snape?"

"At three forty-five. There's a bit of property I have my eye on, but I believe, I *believe* there may be a flaw in the title, a thing I've learned to be wary of. Why you people can't adopt the Australian Torrens System of titling..."

"And you left him?"

"Oh, we got through the details in a matter of twenty minutes."

"And then?"

"I left in the usual way, strolled back to the office and dictated to my secretary until ten thirty: the Board wanted an urgent report as per usual about something totally unpredictable. If you knew the loads of bumf that have plagued me in my time. Even when I was in the Desert I got a signal through to submit a list of all pending typhoid shots, and that with the Eyeties giving us hell."

"I see," said Harry miserably and explained: "He had four visitors in the afternoon—the only visitors there were—and though the switchboard girl marks entries in a notebook, departures are ignored and she cannot swear to anyone having gone out."

"Stone the crows," said Ralf, "you don't suspect me of having concealed meself under Snape's bloody desk?"

"We think the killer could—and it is just a hypothesis—have concealed himself in the building. It's a dim old place."

"You are dead right, an old rabbit warren. I've often thought that if the Home Guard had realised how much of England is old rabbit warrens and the Germans had invaded..."

"Quite." Harry wondered if anybody ever let the little

man finish a sentence, except perhaps the unfortunate troops under his command, and those had been Australians!

"Quite. Do I take it you know the building?"

With the sudden switch to the succinct he achieved when business was mentioned, Ralf said: "Until eight years ago the Snapes rented that place from Chas Fennel, had done so for a hundred odd years. Chas wanted to know did I want it for the company or should we sell it to Snape for eighteen thousand pounds. The Fennels had always hung on to it because they thought it might become valuable, one of their mistakes. Town planning, the drift away from the Cathedral, saw to that. I went round it thoroughly with a surveyor. Fabric well kept up—it was a repairing lease—but not, but definitely not our pigeon. Snape paid cash. I know the building, having a pretty good memory for maps, but why the hell should I kill Snape? Besides, there was somebody coming to see him after I left."

Which meant nothing, decided Harry, having looked at deceased's large appointment pad with its flamboyant legible writing so easy to read.

"He was your solicitor, Mr Fennel?"

He shrugged. "Charles is head of the family. He liked a bit of work—not the business but private work, including service contracts—put in Snape's way. *Noblesse oblige.* No thanks." He declined a cigarette and produced a pouch and rolled one for himself, working dexterously with one hand. "I never can get used to tailor-made somehow. Well, Snape was shrewd and it was always said, 'Go and see Snape', if you asked anybody. Only thing," he lit his old flint and tinder lighter and puffed until the limpish cylinder became alight, "only thing is that I did not like Snape. There were stories that he was not scrupulous in a sly way."

"Where did you hear them?"

"You are the police officer," Fennel gave the Chief Inspector a straight look, "and I do not want to put anybody in. I gossip and listen to a bit of gossip. In my opinion he might have been a crook or something a bloody sight near it. But, well I owe everything I have to Charles and he liked Snape. I mean you may disagree with the skipper, but he knows best. Charles is Chairman of the Conservative Association and Snape was in line for the candidacy."

The Chief Inspector rubbed his chin. "The picture I have is not of an embryo statesman."

"In Court or on a political platform Gerald Snape was well above average and on the latter his personality changed. He could play merry hell—literally, because the old ladies from the Primrose League fair bust their corsets—with a heckler, but at the same time do a warm keep-the-home-fires-burning and help-people-on-fixed-income line.

Harry thanked and got rid of him."

The last person, Harvey Blairs, was a big booming fifty-year-old drum of an estate agent. He had visited Snape at four thirty with a pile of printed forms of contract, remaining until five forty as there was a lot to be done. He had known Snape for fifteen years.

"I did not like him," his eyes were hard, "but people felt safe if Snape was involved in the transaction. We get a client who has not got a solicitor, so we tell him that if he likes Snape will act and name the fee entailed."

"Why did you not like him?"

"Smarmy, sarcastic, creeping up behind you. I'm an honest auctioneer and agent," he grinned, "but I have my ethics. I suspect the late Snape had none. If you are looking for motive, I have not got one. In fact Snape put me on to one or two little things in the way of estates being liquidated as a *quid pro quo* for the business I brought in. I only met him socially a couple of times, our sets being different. I did make a statement the other day. After leaving him I had a whisky in the Deacon's Arms, then took the car back to the office. My secretary and the two colts who assist me were still polishing apples for teacher. The time was six thirty: I told them to push off, closed the door and went home. I have a housekeeper who let me in and prepared my dinner. After eating it I went to the Club and played in a billiard Calcutta from nine thirty until eleven: then to bed and book, both my own. Right?"

"Seems like you will remain at liberty," said Harry, his hand momentarily masked with a great, sweatily sincere handshake. He rather felt he would prefer not to buy a house from Harvey Blairs Esq.

After a quiet personal cup of coffee, he rang for Honeybody, who had been listening over the little intercom, naive people being reassured by the lack of witnesses.

"What do you think?"

"Can't think what you're after—Skipper, as Ralf with an F would say. I'd say we were at Tobruk with no ammunition. It's on the files, he went dutifully back to the office and dictated to his secretary, Miss Taylor, so he's out. I feel it in my bones that this is destined to be on the 'permanent open' file."

The file of unsolved murders was never officially closed.

"I think somebody is lying, perhaps one of the people I saw. I'm going to arrange about this ruddy Inquest. Poke around, will you? What kind of people are they?"

"I can tell you a name for your Cold."

"That's superficial: I want something deeper."

"Right, Harry, old Honeybody will don his Freudian thinking cap forthwith."

"Funny man," said the Chief Inspector as the Sergeant

opened the door, mock-saluted, and lumbered out leaving behind him the faint odour of beer. He had had no time for drinking, Harry could have sworn: perhaps it exuded from his pores after all these years.

In charge of the Inquest was nominally the Superintendent, though to be on the safe side the Chief Constable had arranged for a barrister-at-law to be briefed by a local solicitor, thus costing the tax-payers a further eighty-odd pounds on top of the several hundred or so spent so far in wages.

They went through the depositions of the witnesses to be called.

" 'Murder by a person or persons unknown' is what we want," said Harry. "The Press will be there in force, judging by the interest."

"I made a decision this morning while you were with the Chief," the Superintendent looked a little shifty.

Trying to trump any ace I have, thought Harry grimly.

"I have subpoenaed Lady Joanna Lambone Pye."

"Excellent, but is any evidence she may have admissible?" Harry was cold. "I thought the call would be a formality."

"My fault entirely," said the Super, advancing the frank admission ploy. "We did not consider Lady Joanna, of course, as ladies like her do not go about sticking knives in solicitors or committing murder by any means."

"There was Penelope Fennel."

"Oh, that was years ago, before they were educated. Lady Joanna went to St Hilda's, a blue-stocking, so I understand, who got some kind of maths prize. And as the Chief gave us to understand Penelope Fennel was not quite out of the top drawer, socially speaking. Anyway the local constable, who is a friend of the cook, phoned in to say that her ladyship left home at seven thirty on the night of Snape's death and did not return until some time in the early hours. The housekeeper, also a friend of the cook, is a woman who is perpetually hearing intruders, running water or escaping gas. She thought she heard a noise at around midnight and prowled about in her nightgown. The door of Lady Joanna's bedroom was open—a quirk of hers about ventilation when she was not occupying it. The housekeeper will swear nobody was at home, her ladyship being one of those lightly snoring types you find among women. I mean," the Super reddened slightly, "my wife does. Men either do not snore or else wake the dead, or so," he hastened to add, "one found in the Army. Anyhow, the housekeeper says she heard her ladyship's Humber drive in at around three a.m. This is not an uncommon occurrence. Perhaps twice a month, the housekeeper thinks, she is out until the wee hours: she is a Scots lady."

"It sounds as though the housekeeper has spleen."

"Possibly. Lady Joanna is embalmed around the eighteen forties mentally, a crackpot about bygone glories, poor lady, which does not endear her to the servants. The House of Lords has lost its glamour and you have to be hail-fellow-well-met to get a favourable image today. With her it is God condescending in a nice way, but still the Almighty. Rouses class consciousness in the servants, so it does."

"What does Lady Joanna say?"

"That we should mind our own business, and various allusions to police states, her ancestry and prurient curiosity."

"Prurience, eh. She was hinting that she was with a gentleman, or would she have said *aristocratic* friend, was that it?"

"She must tell under oath," said the Super. "Our barrister, Charles Ingle, has teeth. She has briefed, via her solicitor, Mr Hewson."

Harry whistled. Hewson was fairly high-priced, but

moderate in his demands, a man who could have been a Q.C. but preferred to remain as he was. Above all, a quiet, reasonable, stone-walling kind of man.*

"Buggered if I like this turn, Super."

The Superintendent shrugged. "Think how nice it would be if we could just prove she had a key to the front door, sneaked in, had words with Snape and stuck him. She would have had to carry the fatal weapon in her clouts, proving premeditation. Money or maybe jealousy or both."

Harry was going to protest about the impossibility of Mrs 1970 carrying even the smallest of knuckle-dusters concealed around her person, when he thought of Penelope Fennel, arrayed so that she could have concealed a small trench mortar if she could have stood the weight.

"What are you grinning at?" asked the Super testily.

"A stray thought, that is all."

They spent an hour going over the Inquest strategy. It was routine expected of them.

Back at the Cottage Harry played with Amanda, ate chicken sandwiches, showered and then lay on the bed with Captain Bradstreet's day book, a folio Victorian affair which was half-way appointment register, half-way ledger. He thought that he might get five hundred words of it for the report. It was a dull record of military duties, lunches, dinners and persistent betting losses. As far as he could make out the Captain had lost five hundred and seventy pounds in the first six months of 1874 on horses and a further two hundred at whist. His total gambling on horses was around two

* See *Death and Mr Prettyman*

thousand pounds and at whist five hundred. A dreary, consistent loser, realised Harry, peering at the mercifully large script, schoolboy and oddly unformed.

For the four months before his death there were sundry references to the Regimental Fund. Typical was "Conferred with Bull re Fund." The Captain was not great on spelling. The last one read: "Division of Regimental Funds. See Bull urgently."

At that moment Elizabeth came in. "Why is the brow furrowed? It's practically got holes in it."

"I have the feeling that Captain Bradstreet and Major Bull were in an equal fiddle over the Regimental Fund. See this?"

"The word 'division' could easily apply to the allocation of bequests from the interest, my sweet."

"I have an uneasy feeling that Bull and Bradstreet had been milking the Fund in collusion. What better a combination than Administrator and Auditor? We encounter it all the time."

"If Bradstreet had been in it, surely Bull would have tried, after his death, to push the whole thing on to him. This he didn't do. Now be a good boy and just proceed as you were. Or let your good wife do it on the lines that any funny business with the accounts on Bradstreet's part made no difference to Bull's motive in killing him. After all, Bradstreet might have been threatening to split to the Colonel."

Watching her go, the Chief Inspector thought it the kind of evening for slippers and a couple of thrillers, a stiff nightcap and early to bed. His long acquaintance with Honeybody assured him that the good Sergeant would hardly appear before an hour after the pubs had closed, perhaps later if new-found friends materialised. An uneasy thought occurred that a jovial Honeybody might bring them home, the Sergeant, according to his wife, having brought very strange people home during a long drinking career. He must be well and truly in bed, lights extinguished, slightly before they closed.

He took some hot milk and biscuits at nine p.m. and changed into pyjamas, watching Elizabeth's tawny head as she typed expertly. He judged it nearly time to retire with his books. Wincing, he heard the sound of a latch-key and Honeybody's portly step. He hesitated a bit too long, gauging that at least the Sergeant was alone, when the door opened and he could hardly flee to bed, which had never seemed so attractive. Usually Honeybody was red and benign at this hour, and red he was but worried with it. Harry's heart fell; there were times when Honeybody's buoyancy landed himself perilously close to difficulties such as being co-respondent, a pursuit not encouraged among members of the Metropolitan Police.

Honeybody sat down heavily. "Hardly a drop has passed 'em and a double Scotch would do very well."

One of the Sergeant's understatements, thought Harry as he slopped over to the built-in bar to comply, for there was a distinct whiff of bitter beer in the air.

"Fair hits the spot bang-on," pronounced his helper after a preliminary gulp. "Well, Harry, our young Mr James Cold is in it up to his chin."

"Oh, my God."

"It was quite easy, or a fluke maybe, but I met an old fellow with arthritis who had been the sports reporter for the Greymouth paper until he retired. Young James' father is one Captain Cold."

"Not the armed forces again," said Harry piteously, "besides the file says he's a gas-meter reader. Surely even Labour does better for Captains, like making them Prime Ministers of Northern Ireland, but perhaps he wasn't in a good regiment."

"Football Captain, for twelve years with the Greymouth Colliers—though the mine itself closed down in 1921. A Southern League team who have never won the local cup, but occasionally get a run in the F.A. Cup and whip up enough support for a few lean years ahead. He was centre half and was always being sent off for using his knees in a way I cannot describe in mixed company...."

It must have been quite an amount of ale which failed to wet Honeybody's lips, thought Harry.

"A vicious man with knobs all over him. Craggy, like a good centre half is. Now he's developed his beer belly, but the rest is wire and whipcord and looks kind of strange, but a nasty gent of sixty and when they're nasty at that age you have to watch 'em. You know how it is with small-town football, the favourites being guaranteed, more or less, the licence of a pub when their cartilages can't be patched any more or the beer finally gets into their wind so that it shows."

Harry nodded.

"The old Captain retired fifteen years ago, just in time to meet young Mr Snape head on. It was a matter of a pub which the Captain took it for granted he was going to get after his retirement after twelve seasons as Captain. At the hearing Snape represented other interests, in fact a bunch of residents who wanted the licence rescinded anyway: the neighbourhood was being redeveloped. Poor Cappy Cold was in the crunch. Snape decided the first thing was to stop a new landlord being licensed so he threw the book at poor old Cold. Forty-nine times sent off the field, on twenty-four of these for striking an opponent and once even for biting. Six months' suspension for physically assaulting the ref by butting him in the stomach. Had he the required even temper to run a pub, enquired Snape, and echo, via the Sessions, had to answer 'no'. Worse was to come. The Captain buried his head in the grog bucket and next afternoon was outside Snape's office shouting at him to come and fight like a man. Fancy saying that to a solicitor," Honeybody snorted in disgust. "The upshot was that the Captain was bound over for a year, which finally put paid to his hopes of getting a licence, but they found him a job reading gas meters."

"Much ill will, I suppose."

"In his cups Cappy would threaten to eat Snape's white liver, but only then. To tell the truth he's a gregarious bloke who is suited by meter-reading and not much of a lover of responsibility, which a publican has to take. Then months ago something else happened. The lady mayoress takes a queen-bee kind of interest in the morals of the ladies who work for the corporation. You know," Honeybody adopted a nauseating falsetto, " 'And when *are* you getting married, dear?' or '*who* is your regular boy friend, dear?' Loathed by all: nosy old bitch! However it came to the queenly eye that the morals of her flock were being threatened by the young wolf, James Cold, so she thought of having a word with his father."

"Oh, Gawd," said Harry, weakening and pouring himself a brandy.

"But Dad's testiness is a byword and he is a corporation employee, so the silly old soul thought of a tactful go-between to have 'a word in season' although for the life of me I never fathom what that means precisely."

"She didn't choose Snape!"

"Not knowing the trouble between them, she did that."

"You'd have thought he would have had the brains to refuse."

"Old Madame Mayor is the boss of the Primrose League,

the Society for the Reintroduction of Capital Punishment, the Covenant of Tory Mothers, the United Empire Society, the League of Modest Maidens and the Heath for Victory Movement. Plus others which I have noted.

"The late Snape, eyes on Westminster, was in no position to refuse such a trifling thing. He got the Captain in and said, bluntly, that unless his son kept himself well buttoned up he had no future as a rent collector (pensionable) for Greymouth City Council. The Captain reacted as could be anticipated and was drunk every night for a week, mouthing about what he was going to do to Snape. Then a week before the murder he turned silent and morose, hardly touching a glass and very savage to anybody who contradicted him."

A beautifully constructed crime, it would have been, thought the Chief Inspector. The son so curiously, yet so convincingly providing an alibi: the girl unable to gainsay it, the father creeping along in stockinged feet, settling Snape before his paralysed legs could get him to his feet, and as stealthily departing.

Elizabeth came back with the whisky decanter and poured for herself and Honeybody. "But has the boy motive?" she said.

"Murder to protect one's chances of rent-collecting?" Harry laughed without humour. "I've known more slender motives. And there have been cases of an obsessional Family Enemy, who sometimes does not realise he is one: suburbia with these brooding hatreds which make best-sellers, but that side of it does exist. My uncle had trouble with his neighbour in 1921, something about a doormat, and they never spoke. Over the years the neighbour, a mild civil servant, became Satan to my uncle. Nothing overt, no rows, just cold silence and glances. It infected me. I thought the neighbour was

Satan for many years, and even my father, a genial man, used to ignore him as they scuttled, bowlers and umbrellas, to catch the eight fifteen. What are the family circumstances?"

"I'll lay a change of clothes out," said Elizabeth resignedly, "because I suppose you'll both be off to police headquarters."

"Cappy Cold is a widower with a rather nice detached house, the gift of a series of efforts made by the supporters club in the year they knocked out Arsenal from the Cup, in a goodish district. He has a motor bike. He and the son live alone, on good terms I gather. There are no more children. The house is sparsely furnished, but clean and tidy. They pay cash, I got that from the little local store." Honeybody looked smug.

"No lodgers or boarders?"

"It's a three-bedroomed job but the Captain keeps the third empty for his football mementoes. Between the two of them they can live quite comfy. The Captain would like the son to bring a wife home before long to do the cooking and housework."

Harry went to dress, forcing away the temptation to take a ten-minute snooze-off. He telephoned the Superintendent, found him ensconced with the Chief Constable (a bit of olde Englishe double-crossing? part of his mind queried) and announced he was coming over urgently.

With something of a pain he said goodbye to Elizabeth, now tucked into a bucket-shaped chair, and to Honeybody, who had found a bowl and was proceeding to make iced punch in it.

Colonel Angel, in a wreath of cigar smoke, was with the Superintendent when Harry arrived to report. The two men listened in heavy silence.

"The girl, presumably the innocent stooge, would be the weak link," said Angel eventually.

"He would see to it that she could swear to nothing," said the Super. "A rattle-pated little brat who should be spanked hard."

"I was thinking, sir, that we should call James Cold. The son, not the father. If we screw the son down, the old man, sharp-tempered as he is, will say something. Neither need we call the girl as yet. Let her remain, poor kid, as the mystery factor."

"All right," said the Chief, "I happen to know our solicitor is at bridge, so it will be my pleasure to summon the poor fellow."

He proved, in half an hour's time, filled by coffee-sipping, to be a brusque old man with a rare capacity to get to the heart of things. In the end he had taken six small notes with which to amend his brief to counsel.

"The 'quest is at ten," he said. "I'm seeing counsel at nine thirty: he arrives at the Grand around midnight. You will see the boy is served with papers?"

"I'll be in at seven," said the Colonel with rectitude, "and will put the machine in operation. Serving is no problem—he'll be one of the pigeons round the Town Hall."

"That seems to be that," said Harry.

"And now," the Colonel glanced at his watch, "perhaps you gentlemen will join me for a nightcap at the Club."

VII

IT HAD BEEN, in fact, four o'clock when the Chief Inspector, with the aid of a taxi, had quit the Chief Constable's little study, with its delightful prints and small but comprehensive library of forensic works. The old gentleman, in an insomniac's heaven, was obviously heading towards a game of chess—the Super and the lawyer had dropped out after the Club had closed—when some inspiration caused Harry to start worrying about his children, an always foolproof gambit as long as you did not keep repeating the same diseases. This time Amanda had an incipient ingrowing toenail.

"At that age, poor little bitch! God knows what she'll be like at fifty"—the Colonel had drink taken—"but I'll ring for a taxi. It won't take long."

He telephoned. Harry guessed that everybody jumped when the Chief wanted something for it seemed only a few minutes before the door-bell rang: but it was the hour of the night when time was still.

"I'm annoyed that my fellers missed the Cold senior angle," said the Chief, extinguishing his cigar butt.

"I'd say that Captain Cold runs generally in anti-copper circles. My man Honeybody is an unknown and has a way with him."

His present way, at eight a.m., with Harry running late and with a knocking sound like a vintage car in his skull, was slavering into three rashers of bacon and a mountain of scrambled egg.

"You must eat! What about a little cold ham and melon?" So came the wifely whine as she wiped Amanda's disgusting chin.

The tomato juice was making its slow acid process down his duodenum and whoever invented coffee wanted their head read. He forced a fixed smile. "Like a tattooist one works better on an empty stomach."

They looked at him blankly.

"Feeling bad?" asked Honeybody.

"I'm all right," he almost snapped, then remembered his determination to Be Pleasant on mornings after, plastered back his smile, kissed his wife and Amanda and went out to the car with what he hoped was stately, businesslike progress, an effect marred when his wife chased after him with his stuffed briefcase.

It would have been a bad morning but for the soothing syrup of the solicitor, the professional calm of the barrister, Mr Charles Ingle. Their rank, Harry gloomily remembered, entitled them to the superscription "Esquire" and to present their wives to the Queen. The Chief Constable was on the bloodshot side, though confessing, reluctantly, to three hours of sleep, and the Superintendent was plainly dyspeptic.

"One thought," said Mr Ingle, "that one was to go for Lady Joanna Lambone Pye, a sitting duck one is afraid. Now we have a lecherous young man, a seated drake one fears. The trouble about double-barrelled shotguns in a court is failure to wound mortally."

"I think it is not shooting but fishing, Mr. Ingle," said the Chief. "We have no evidence against anybody. I had a word with the Coroner. He'll go along with us within limits."

"What limits?"

"I told him we are not calling Jane Smithers nor do we

wish to introduce any sexual element, just the facts. Where was Lady Joanna Lambone Pye? Did this wretched youth actually hear nothing?"

"It would be interesting to know where his father was," said Charles Ingle.

"The local constable," said the Superintendent, "says that Captain Cold either spends his evenings at home, frequently alone, going through his press-cutting book, or else at the nearby pub being gregarious among the old-time sportsmen of his generation. We keep an eye on the pubs, as usual, but the local man has no idea whether Cold was there on the night in question or not. Local pubs are the same every night, more or less, and it is the very devil of a job to authenticate anything."

Charles Ingle made a note. "No objection if I ask the son where his father was that night?"

"Can you bring it in?"

"With some ingenuity I can, if the Coroner's not adverse. A doctor, isn't he?"

The Chief Constable nodded. Generally policemen prefer medically trained coroners rather than legally trained ones. The local deputy coroner was a decent old G.P. In fact the knowledge of law which a coroner requires could be assimilated by any moderately brainy twelve-year-old in a three-months crash course. The medical side was a different matter, thought Harry, possibly requiring six months.

They made their way to the Grey Goat, where the Coroner's Room had been perfunctorily dusted. "They say," confided the Chief Constable, "that an eccentric coroner in the eighteen forties used to have the corpse laid out on the billiard table with crossed cues on its chest: a merry old bird by all accounts."

There was a crowd, about twenty gentlemen of the Press,

seated hunched on hard chairs, an equal number of the public crowded on forms of the type used in schools, and a few dignitaries flanking the Coroner. Harry, seating himself at the solicitors' table, saw Sir Charles Fennel's blond, florid face seated next to the Mayor, a worried, small man who took things seriously, including his wife, a formidable lady next to him with a remarkable hat. The Coroner, a comfortable-looking fellow with a vast, crinkled elderly face like a small cushion, came in at four minutes past ten. He swore in a jury of ten, sensible-looking men who appointed a bank teller (so the Chief told Harry) as their foreman.

Diffidently the Coroner said that if the Jury desired to see deceased he had him ready, but that they need not, an escape which was unanimously accepted except for one mousy-looking man who looked a trifle on the wistful side but was shut up.

The inevitable Home Office pathologist opined that death had been instantaneous with little emission of blood and had occurred at approximately nine p.m., but give or take half an hour.

Mr Hewson (for Lady Joanna Lambone Pye): "Could it not be an hour or two hours either way? Are you taking into account the humidity of the particular night?"

The pathologist: "I have the temperature of the cadaver taken next morning by the police surgeon."

Mr Hewson: "The initial fall in temperature is very slow, is it not too rash to make such statements unless there is very precise evidence of room temperature?"

The pathologist: "I adhere to my opinion. I examined the cadaver within fourteen hours of death."

Charles Ingle (for the Greymouth Police): "In the course of your practice you have examined how many corpses to establish time of death?"

Harry had been vaguely thinking how young the pathologist was. But you have to start: there is a point in his career where a surgical student, flying on his own, sticks his first incision into some innocent patient, carefully watched by Matron who could do it far better herself.

"Three," said the pathologist, guilty. Ingle recoiled.

"Did they all pass away at nine p.m. precisely?" asked Mr Hewson.

"Now," said the Coroner sternly. "Witness' opinion is a quite valid one, whether his experience is of three or three hundred, er, um, unfortunate people."

"About death," it was the mousy-looking juror. "We know all about heart transplants and the controversy. Are you sure he was *dead*?"

"His heart was stuck through with a kitchen knife and immediately ceased to function." The pathologist was red in the face but patient.

"Is not there a question of that brain?" pressed the juryman. "Does it not go on ticking as it were?"

"Without blood there are no electrical impulses in the brain within a comparatively short time. In traumatic cases—instances of accident—we assess death at the time the heart ceases to beat, which in this case is clearly at the moment of the stabbing."

"But the spiritual side," persisted the mousy man, "is something that my Pastor is dissatisfied about. Are you saying that the late Mr Snape's soul departed from this Vale of Tears at approximately nine p.m.?"

The acute embarrassment of the medical profession when confronted with theology (the pathologist's ultimate boss was a lay preacher) showed itself in witness' face, but the Coroner smoothly went up to bat. "We are here, sir, to render unto Caesar as it were. Doubtless the Almighty, in His wisdom, could answer the questions you propound. Perhaps sir, earnest prayer may be called for the meditation, but for the moment we are busy men with limited time."

Altogether, thought the Chief Inspector, the Coroner had handled it admirably, but with one little snide remark Hewson had rather destroyed the value of the evidence, though the High Court would be something else again.

The partners gave evidence that Snape had been immersed in business at six o'clock and there was no cross-examination. The staff was a different matter. Hewson established that there had originally been twelve keys cut to the front door: the chief clerk could only account for eight with any certainty and Chief Inspector James cursed himself for not having double-checked on the local police. He made a note. It was a hole to be patched or cobbled up before criminal proceedings—one of the reasons, in fact, why the police favoured Inquests and defending counsel loathed them.

"Lady Joanna Lambone Pye," called the usher. You had to admit, thought Harry, that whatever your social views a few generations of upper-class living did in many cases, though by no means all, produce a kind of dignity. Darkly beautiful, she knew enough of her faults to consciously relax the rat-trap grip of her mouth as she took her seat.

"Lady Joanna," said Charles Ingle, "you knew Mr Snape?"

"Seven years ago we founded a few small companies dealing in investments. To that extent we were acquaintances."

"And sometimes you ate together?"

"We have eaten together at public restaurants. I dare say that over the years Mr Snape had lunched at my home on several occasions."

"Did he never come to dinner?"

"I could not swear one way or the other. Generally I hold a dinner for friends once a month. Mr Snape may have been invited."

"Without offence, Lady Joanna, is it true that you were engaged to deceased or had some understanding?"

"Mr um, our relationship was purely a matter of business."

"Quite so. And you used to visit him at his office?"

"Yes."

"At night and when the staff had gone, he used to leave open the side door in the alleyway."

"Quite often, say twice per month."

"And did you visit him on the night of the twenty-eighth?"

There was a small silence. The Chief Inspector remembered the other woman who, nearly a hundred years before, had sat in this same room, doubtless as shabby and seedy then as now, facing counsel. Charles Ingle, however, was bound by courtesies and reticences unknown to a lustier age.

"Certainly not!" Her contralto, too harsh for a woman, it seemed to Harry, was disdainful.

"Is it true that you declined to tell the police where you were on the night in question?"

"Yes."

"Did you leave home at six?"

"I left home at six, more or less, and returned at three the next morning. I decline to say where I was except that it was nowhere near Snape's place of business. Perhaps that will cut short your questions."

Mr Ingle gave a little bow. In a Coroner's Court there is no embargo against leading a witness in direct examination and he said: "Are you protecting somebody?"

"Yes."

"Not yourself?"

"No."

"Have you ever possessed a kitchen knife?"

"My servants may. I do not know what kitchen implements I possess. I am not a cook."

"I am sure your ladyship would be a most competent one. Please listen, were your relations with Mr Snape always amiable?"

"They were about money. One always disagrees about money. He was always trying to reduce my percentage of the profits. But I bore him no malice for that: he was a business man. Ours was a mutually profitable association, his death will be a loss not a gain for me."

Ingle hitched his own gown and turned to business.

"You and deceased were in fact money-lenders."

"You put it in a markedly unpleasant way. We were investors. Often we advanced certain sums against security. We had a lot of second mortgages, among other things."

"What is outstanding?"

Snape's Estate would be damned lucky to get much back from Lady Joanna, thought the Chief Inspector. She said quite smoothly, "It was as much as fifty thousand pounds at peak periods. At his death we had run down commitments to around seven thousand."

"Could we have details?"

"Mr Coroner, any details would be possibly harmful to the business, to me and to Mr Snape's heir. Besides which they are confidential money matters calculated to cause embarrassment to people quite unconnected with this murder."

Ingle continued to press, hampered by the fact that he was purely fishing in the hope of catching something. Twice the Coroner checked him.

When it ended Hewson said urbanely: "Lady Joanna, I think we might be quite frank. Did you not spend the night with a certain gentleman?"

"I did."

"And public scrutiny of this might damage him?"

"There are reasons why I should not reveal his name."

Ingle, half rising, said: "Protecting his honour?"

"Mr Coroner," said Hewson, "in this day and age surely a woman may protect a man's honour. For all we know the consequences of her mentioning the name might be grave indeed."

"Mr Hewson," said the Coroner, "counsel for the police has obliged your client by not quite forcing her into the position of committing contempt of this court. I am content to leave it at that. I do not have to warn her that conceivably she might be a witness before one of Her Majesty's judges when the result of her refusal might be decidedly unpleasant."

"Thank you, sir." Hewson sat down, still winning comfortably on points, even if at the expense of his client's reputation. But it did not matter in this permissive age, thought Harry. In Penelope's day women quite literally were found guilty of murder on the evidence of sexual laxity. Today it was nothing. Nobody would strike Lady Joanna off the eligible-for-dinner list. She would probably find her name on many more, and if she wanted she could write a column for a magazine or two.

"Mr James Cold," said the usher.

The young man looked nervous and ratty. Where he had been sitting was somebody who could well be his father, with the rather battered face that old pro athletes inevitably collect, a monumental paunch and wide, bony shoulders. He looked the kind of man who was never far from his next drink and with the irritable, dyspeptic manner of one suffering from alcoholic gastritis.

Ingle proceeded to slaughter the son while Hewson doodled on his scratch-pad.

Cold, sweating, admitted that he had entered—without permission—a large closet within the side entrance of Snape's office and had lain on the floor during the relevant time.

"What were you doing on the floor?" asked Mr Ingle.

"What was I doing?"

"I dare say you can understand English. Where did you go to school?"

"Greymouth Mixed Modern."

"Then you can speak it, so what were you doing?"

"Talking," said Cold, in some despair.

"Lying on the floor talking. To yourself?"

"To a friend."

"I see. But you did the talking, not the friend."

"I s'pose you might put it that way."

"And the friend would not be in a position to hear footsteps?"

"Ask my friend."

"I have not called her for the reason of her reputation," said Mr Ingle, sanctimoniously and ignoring his examination of Lady Joanna. "But could she have heard footsteps: was not your conversation brilliant enough to stop her ears?"

"I suppose you are right."

"You left at ten thirty, leaving the door as you found it. When did you get home?"

"I walked my friend home. It's about half a mile from me. I got the late-night bus, say twelve forty-five when I used the latch key."

"Your father was up?"

"He..." Cold stopped. He had been going quite well

really, his attention diverted to Miss Jane Smithers. Now, in the classic way, Ingle had jerked the rope.

"He," said Cold, "well, I dunno."

"Was not Mr Snape trying to get you the sack?"

"He had me in for a talk."

"About what?"

"A bit of assing about at work, being cheeky to the girls. Nothing at all."

"This is a permissive society, no doubt, but you had gone a bit out of bounds, eh? Some complaints were made."

"Harmless fun can be taken two ways, you know."

"Particularly if it results in conversation on the floor of closets. Do you know what criminal conversation is?"

"No, sir."

"Sometimes known as adultery, Mr Cold. Now obsolete. But you were saying that the married ladies so objected to your advances that Mr Snape had a word with you, telling you to behave yourself."

"I think," said the Coroner, "that unless we have a cogent reason we might not proceed with this line of examination."

(*What Happened in the Closet?* the horrible old lady who represented the *Bulletin* was writing in her notebook. *Coroner Does Not Proceed*, wrote *The Times*.)

"I would hope, Mr Coroner, that in perfect fairness I could introduce evidence to the effect that the witness had no cause to like deceased."

"I see no reason why you should."

"I accept your learned ruling, sir. In other words, Mr Cold, it was a paternal conversation, eh? Doubtless Mr Snape was an old friend of your father and gave you a word in season. Perfectly understandable."

James Cold stood silent and impaled.

"Well..."

"Not a friend of your father?"

"Well..."

"An enemy of your father?"

"He was an effing, silk-worm-looking bastard," shouted the man Harry had picked as Cold's father. "A money-lending old turd of gigantic dimensions. A crawling son-of-a-bitch. But I didn't do him neither."

"I think we should take this gentleman's evidence," said Charles Ingle, smoothly.

"I don't think..." said the Coroner, plainly wishing he had stuck to people with internal trouble on national health.

"I demand to be sworn. Get down off that platform, sonny, and let your pa have a go."

Mr Ingle stared down at his hands.

"Now, Dad," said James Cold, "there's no need to carry on like that, I'm sure."

"I have me rights, touching the death of Gerald Snape, that you were sworn in to testify. I won't have my reputation took, as I told the Football Association in 1960. Kicking in the crutch I never did, the knee perhaps when strongly provoked, and I admit once I bit a centre forward. I can't say fairer than that."

"If you will get off the box, Mr Cold, I suppose I shall have to swear your father."

The Captain proved to be one Albert Cold, roughly twice as large as his son.

"I will make it very quick," said Charles Ingle. "What were you doing the night that Mr Snape was killed?"

"Walking," said the Captain. "The boy and I live alone since the wife died. The TV was horrible. I was nervous. Oh, I admit that Snape's threat to have the boy chucked out upset me. At ten I went out and walked. When I was in training I thought nothing of running six miles. That evening I walked until one-ish, say ten miles, sweating out the bottled beer. The boy was probably in bed when I got in, had a bite of cheese and a whisky and turned in."

"You saw nobody?"

"I was in a black mood." The Captain almost snarled his answer. "One of those moods when you do not see anybody."

"You did not know what you were doing, in fact?"

"Now look here," said the Captain, "I have you swearing my life away. A man can go for a walk, can't he, to sweat out the God-awful bottled beer they make these days?"

"You did not like the late Gerald Snape?"

"I've said what I think of him."

"Which did not appear to be much. Do you drink at the Lord Collingwood?"

"That's my pub, my local."

"You did not get drunk there and then go to see Mr Snape?"

"As God is my judge I did not."

(No evidence to the contrary, thought Harry, watching Charles Ingle.)

"Did you ever notice that the late Mr Snape doodled things on his blotter?"

"I do not know."

"You had been in his office several times?"

"Three times to my memory."

"Would it surprise you to learn that on his blotter—and he used a clean sheet of paper each day—was written the word *Collingwood*?"

Captain Cold sweated in silence. Harry's eyes sought those of the Superintendent, who was engrossed in reading a document. You could hardly blame him for wanting to wipe

Scotland Yard's eye, though it was naughty. The Super glanced momentarily sideways and blushed as he caught the Chief Inspector's eye.

Ostentatiously Harry left the Court, having no evidence himself to give, and took a seat in the "lounge", carefully ordering a dry ginger ale. On the whole he bore the Superintendent no malice: the man was probably after the Chief Constableship in due course. He asked the landlord, who was in a state of nerves, explained, he said, by the strain of having corpses around the place: "Have you an encyclopaedia?"

Pubs always have encyclopaedias, issued by newspapers in the nineteen thirties and donated by the breweries. He chose his volume, bound in rexine, now slightly fly-blown, with tarnished golden printing upon it.

He was studying it when Honeybody arrived.

The Sergeant ordered a lemonade with a ghastly look of distaste.

"The double-cross fell through, Harry. They called the landlord of the pub and he could not tell whether Cappy Cold was in the rubbidy that night or not. You know how it is."

The Chief Inspector did. A man who goes into a public house regularly has a kind of floating alibi, because nobody can ever be produced to swear that he was not there on the date in question. Murder trials are won or lost, generally lost, on such evidence.

"What Mr Ingle was up to try to prove was that Cold had rung Snape up to mention that he would be in the pub at, say, eight p.m. and would then come along. Snape was a compulsive doodler on his blotter. Cold denied everything. However Ingle did well to get the evidence in at all. The

Coroner's winding up now. 'Murder by person or persons unknown'."

"I knew it in my bones," said Harry, "we should have put in for an adjournment. Now we'll simply have more and more pressmen breathing down our necks. I think we'd better go before it starts."

"One of Elizabeth's dry martinis would be nice," agreed Honeybody.

They were getting into the car, in the jammed little park, when Harry groaned. One of the older school of journalists, he thought, who had his permanent niche in the Press Club as one of the "characters". There was a certain impecunious impression as from one who backed horses unsuccessfully and bought clothes at the sales, overlain by a bright, sandy-haired kind of vitality. A bachelor, thought Harry, looking at the badly washed drip-dry shirt.

"I hear you are the Yard man," said the newcomer, rather diffidently, not in character.

"What paper?"

"Paper. Oh, I see, but I'm not newspapers. I work in Covent Garden, but not the publishing parts. Spanish melons and green peppers is what we do."

"Have you information?"

"Can you give me a lift? My car is parked down the road and I do not want to hang around."

Harry opened the back door, let the stranger in, drove out of the park and jinked through various back streets. He stopped in a quiet road.

"My name is Ted Gould," said the man. "We and the Fred Smiths have a kind of monopoly over names." He gave a rather nervous laugh. "I was in the back of the Court. I think she saw me . . . the Lady Joanna I mean."

"So she saw you."

"She was sleeping with me the night this fellow Snape got his packet. I've a flat off Charing Cross Road. She comes up once a fortnight."

"Why didn't she say so?"

"She's ashamed of me," said Ted Gould. "She is a pukka lady, the family had native servants and whips and that lot. I met her at a point-to-point. I was driving down South and the pubs had shut. Somebody told me there was a Spanish champagne tent under special licence at this riding business. She picked me up. Three years ago. I'm beneath her in a manner of speaking. A fine lady as you might say, in every way. She despises me, but we get along. A pity that Wilson and his lot are going to abolish her, but that's the way the game goes. She'd die rather than admit she was cuddling a dirty old working-class man like me."

"Hanging's abolished," said the Chief Inspector.

"More's the pity," said Ted Gould, shrewdly, "that and flogging was the best aphodisiac the old country ever had. I've read books about it."

"If you are faking this, Mr Gould, you will not get away with it and the consequences will be serious."

"I've never been in trouble, except once for being drunk and twice getting girls into trouble in my teens, so the record is clean. I don't know I could prove Jo was in my flat *that* night, but you can't keep these things dark and over the years people know her by sight. I can prove she was in the habit of coming up to the flat, and then it will be my word against everybody else's."

"Take a short statement, Sergeant, quite voluntarily given. Just name, address, and the hours when Lady Joanna was there, according to recollection."

Honeybody obliged and Harry subsequently dropped Gould near his car.

"That would be that," observed Honeybody.

"Unless a bribed professional witness," grumbled Harry annoyed.

"I wouldn't put it past her," said Honeybody, "but he's not the type. Just a public-house stud with no real guts like you have to have with perjury. I'll have him checked. I suppose we now hie to the pub. Dare say Captain Cold and his youthful will take a little restorative and rest of the day off work."

"Let me see," Harry talked aloud as he drove slowly, checking street names, "the inference is that perhaps Cold senior had arranged to phone Snape from the Collingwood, or even to meet him outside it. But why?"

"Cappy Cold is no mug. Suppose he had found something out regarding Snape, a man with a lot of little secrets, a lot which he would not want flourished in the light of day. Perhaps he told Snape to meet him outside the Collingwood, went into the office, waited until his son and the girl came along as alibis, then produced the knife. Foolproof."

"But with too many loose ends as yet, and the time factor is not very good. Still..."

"But have you got anything better?" persisted the Sergeant.

"I thought so at the beginning, but have lost a bit of faith on the way. I think the locals, fearing they'd have to call us in, were a bit slack on the full detail work."

"The file looks on that side, but you cannot blame them."

The Collingwood had been put up just before the brewers grew arty as well as crafty and was a large featureless place on a corner: bright and comfortable enough inside and with three bars.

"Not here yet," said Honeybody at length, "but, oh God, look who is."

Ralf Fennel beamed and beckoned over his bitter and double roast sandwich which he assured them was a speciality of the house and contained both crackling and good stuffing.

"Talking of stuffing, sir," said the Sergeant slowly, "I'll treat myself, I think."

"Me too," said his superior, stepping on his toe. "Bit off your beat," he added with the idle professional curiosity of the copper as he beckoned to the barmaid.

"No, no, on me. On me. My friends will join me, miss. No, Sir Charles owns the freehold. Not interested in pubs is he, poor soul, so looking after it as Director is yours truly. A pleasant little chore and the Manager is a good fellow."

(Who patiently puts up with your endless talk, thought Harry.)

But the pork was good and they had a similar round, discovering in the process that Ralf knew an astonishing lot of useless information about breeding pigs.

"Can I drop into your office this afternoon?" asked Harry casually.

"About four I shall be free."

"It's just that we are checking on you four who saw him in the afternoon. It'll be a case of your secretary."

"She's a wizard," said Ralf, "dunno what I'd do without her."

"Here come our customers," said Honeybody.

Looking up the Chief Inspector saw the Colds enter, the father looming over the son, his belt down beneath the swag belly.

"You're welcome, old boy, a nasty pair I believe."

"And 'oo might you be," asked Cappy Cold with the ponderous sarcasm of a man who rather relishes a punch up.

"They're the two 'tecs down from the Yard. Decent sorts,

though you did"—James Cold could not keep from lapsing into a whine for very many minutes—"say that I would not be called at the 'quest."

"It was the locals who decided to put you up," said Harry not altogether truthfully, as he swiftly paid for a round of pints and pork sandwiches, momentarily thinking of the herds of pigs the customers must go through in a good month.

"Well, I said you were a gentleman."

"I got a bit mad at the questions, I'm sorry to say. It was like a ref I had good cause to butt, he being so unfair. You see red, you know, and then, lo and be'old, you find you've upset people." Cappy Cold talked around his sandwich.

"I know exactly how it is, old man, but doubt whether you did justice to yourself."

"Doubt I did what?" The pale eyes had turned hard again and blood suffused the lantern face with its two hairy moles and four grog blossoms.

"Do you know that most people don't?"

"Eh." The "do's" momentarily fogged Cappy as Honeybody inconspicuously leaned on his left heel, the ham-like left fist which had once put him in line for Olympic selection lightly on his waist.

"I mean," said Harry, "nobody doubts your word, but as you say in the heat of the moment and getting confused things can come out incorrectly: and it's important to get it put right immediately."

He was working it out when his son whined: "He says you can get the statement put right immediately. He's a white man, Dad."

Eventually Cappy Cold got the point. As Honeybody had surmised he was basically no idiot. He gained time when a small, apple-cheeked gentleman came from the entrance to the public intent upon the toilet. But he saw Cold and paused: "Don't often see you in this field, Cappy."

"I have," the Captain's face flushed again, "a bit of private business."

"Ar," said the little man as he went and bestowed a valedictory in the direction of Honeybody's belly, "for twelve years, sir, Cappy was the idol of our town. The idol of our town."

Rather mollified by the turn of events, Cappy bought a round, adorned with the inevitable sandwiches, which were beginning to lie heavily on their bed of stuffing in the Chief Inspector's stomach. Eventually he said: "Would it surprise you to learn that I was protecting a lady's honour?"

Beer got into Honeybody's nose: Harry bit back the words which came to his lips before thinking quickly and saying, face within hitting distance of Cappy's strong breath: "Suppose you tell me about it, sir, while we have another sandwich and a drop of Scotch to wash it down."

"Do it, Dad," pleaded the younger Cold while the Chief Inspector ordered.

They ate in silence until Cappy wiped his upper lip. "She's a lady, sir. The hubby is a bookie in a nice way of business. He goes to London when the fights are on ... and I, well I would not want you to think she is anythink but a very modest, dainty girl, sir. I get on my bike and cycle round about seven. The night Snape got done I was home after the young hopeful 'cause I saw his light on as I came in without making no noise."

"Do you eat or have a drink, sir?"

"She does me proud, sir. It was a buck rarebit and half a bottle of red wine she gave me. But her name cannot cross my lips, sir. Old Snape was a pinch of poo in trousers, but while I might have kicked him or bashed him on his little snout, I would never stick a bit of cold steel into anybody. There's probably ten thousand people in the county who saw Cappy Cold in his prime. They're his reference. I never kicked a player who'd got crippled a minute previous though you see some rotters do that every day. Ethics is what it's called and the young 'uns frankly do not have it now."

Overcome by events, the Chief Inspector put down his half-consumed sandwich, assured Cappy Cold he would do what he could and made for the door and the car.

He fiddled with ignition key and said: "Do you think they are *all* lying?"

The Sergeant thriftily finished the corner of his sandwich: "A very nice piece of pork. Not that that sort of thing is a real meal. All lying? I never met a case where they all did. Say seventy-five per cent as a good average. What the deuce were the Colds doing in the Saloon? From what the little man said, their roost is the Public. And why were they co-operative? I incline to think there was a woman, Harry, there always is with a fellow like Cappy. It would have been more in character for him to shut up and come out with it later to sue for wrongful arrest arising out of malice or carelessness. And the son was backing him up. It was very much the case of changing spots."

"We've got four people to see," said Harry. "I'll see Ralf Fennel's secretary and dodge the gentleman with the F. You drop me and drive the car home. I'll taxi back. Any meetings with the Chief can be, shall be," he grinned, "left until tomorrow."

It was only three when he reached Fennel's outer office. The small man was in conference, would not be free until four.

"It's rather you I wanted to see, Miss, er," he glanced at the painted name tag on the desk, "Taylor. What time did

Mr Fennel return here on the afternoon of the twenty-sixth?"

"Ten past four, give or take a minute or two."

"And he left?"

"He was in his inner office until ten thirty. Most of the time he was dictating an urgent draft of a report. He could not tape it because of its intricate nature. There is only one way out and that is through here. I only left on one occasion for a few minutes."

"Australian aren't you?" he smiled.

"Adelaide originally."

Nearing forty, thought Harry expertly, and very attractive in a cool way.

"I'm up to my furry ears," he said, "so do us a favour. Just type it, date and sign so I can just put it in the file."

"A pleasure." Her nimble fingers flickered over the keyboard of the electric typewriter. She got out an envelope, signed the top sheet and carbons. "Four carbons for you, plus original, one carbon for us here."

He thanked her and left, walking through the hot sunlight back to the Cathedral Square and a philosophic old man in a battered cab.

Mr Bones, feeling neglected, momentarily beat his feet against the Chief Inspector's chest, but the children had mercifully undergone the process known as "potting and putting down". The big table in the work-room was covered with neat piles of copy paper. Elizabeth's skill at the typewriter, once good, was now rusty, but Sir Charles Fennel insisted that their draft be typed by her and not by any local. Eventually, Harry supposed, fair copies would be made in London by specialist agencies and delivered to the writer who was to dress it up for publication. Sir Charles, or rather his wife, was sparing no money, even unto twelve pages of colour plates and thirty-two in monochrome. It would be typical moneyed luck, observed Harry as he sat down, if the thing sold fifty thousand and made good money.

"It's a wonderful story," said Elizabeth, "as we've got the synopsis and everything. The poor lady, pregnant by a bankrupt double-crossing cad, is wrongly accused, driven mad and to her death, while the culprit was the embezzling Major Bull. I do not think we should allude to the possibility of collusion between Bradstreet and Bull, because Lady Fennel is one who likes a good straight, uncomplicated story line like Gore Vidal does." Elizabeth had become quite friendly with Lady Fennel over various cups of tea and one cold lunch.

"Seated in that ruddy court," said Harry, "where Penelope Fennel was nearly a century ago, listening to a crowner, a competent one this time thank heaven, investigate an equally inexplicable murder I just got a feeling that our Penny narrowly escaped falling into the right slot—the one a hangman would jerk open."

"Now," said his wife, "I suspect that the Fennels are getting us on the cheap."

"It was either this or that ghastly house in Clacton with my cousin talking of the Great Pyramid and getting bloater paste over her moustache. Whichever way you calculate it, we're a hundred pounds ahead over this, plus a lot of free grog and eggs and garden truck."

"What the Fennels want is to be able to say that the innocence of Penelope is right in the opinion of an eminent Yard detective, anonymous of course. Lady Fennel let her hair down at lunch a bit after those two swift martinis she took. It's not your time, Harry, it's the years of study and experience. You remember the story..."

"Yes, yes," snarled her husband, who abhorred the cliché

anecdote, "but I've made my arrangement and cannot go whining for more payment. Let me get to work."

He had cheese sandwiches at the table at eight o'clock, hardly looking up from his work. At nine Honeybody came in.

"All those alibis I looked at are okay, Harry, so I won't bother Elizabeth, but just nick over to the Grey Goat. Join me later?"

"Come in for a moment, Sarge," Harry was very formal as he got up and walked to the door and called towards the lounge room:

"Leave us alone for a bit, will you, old girl?"

They sat on opposite sides of the cluttered table. "I'm either going to make a prize fool of myself or notch up some seniority with this one. The way we are going I can *smell* that we're going into one of those alleys you dream you are driving along, where the walls imperceptibly draw in until finally, zonk, you're immovably stuck."

Honeybody only dreamed of women on the large side, his wife being skinny, but he was familiar with the neurotic side of the Chief Inspector's nature. Big fat people in his experience dreamed more normally than shortish, thinnish ones. But he nodded ingratiatingly.

"And I have a hunch. I do not want to get the bird from the Super here."

Sensitive about his new rank, experience told the Sergeant, who without comment walked to the small cabinet in the corner and poured two largish Scotches.

"That will do you good, Mr James. I must say that in the last murder case we made a little bit of an error* but as a working record your hunches are better than anybody's."

* *A Death in the Church*

"Just listen to me." The Chief Inspector talked for half an hour. Honeybody refilled the glasses.

"I take your word for the facts, Mr James. I think it probably must have happened that way, but we'll have to dig."

"Which is what you are going to do. Tomorrow you take the car—I can hire another—and take off for Victoria Street. I'll get Hawker in a moment and start it. You know the facts and the people—I'll make a précis for you. You'll sit in London and keep me posted every six hours—I won't phone *you* because nobody can chain you to a desk during opening hours."

"Have I a free hand?"

"I don't want trivialities referred to me. And Superintendent Hawker will certainly not want to get particularly involved, or not to the extent that he cannot wash his hands of it. As far as boozing, well you have to ascertain whether the Suspect has any London affiliations. We cannot say yes or no at the moment. I do not mean business connections, which exist as we know they do; but criminal ones."

"Is the Suspect a criminal?" rumbled the Sergeant.

"That will come when we get fingerprints"—Harry made a note. "The usual 'Can you help me with this address?' with a sensitised envelope to hold. Tomorrow I'll put it on an afternoon train and notify you. I rather think the killer would be an ex-con because it is a calculated crime of some ingenuity."

"So in the meantime," said Honeybody, "I'll pack my traps and go out for a final round at the pub."

VIII

THE FOLLOWING FOUR days were busy ones for Chief Inspector James, yet an odd lack of purpose seemed apparent to the Chief Constable, who had discreetly rung Hawker. No complaints, mind you, but perhaps a senior man was needed. Alas, Hawker was non-committal, bemoaning the lack of men senior to him to act as guide to the Chief Inspector.

What the aged Superintendent had done after replacing his handset was to tap his spatulate finger ends on his desk for several seconds. As he was a protégé, Hawker did not mind seeing Chief Inspector James rake up a bit of kudos, but the old man liked his share of the loot. On the other hand, James was now advanced enough in his career, Hawker considered, to take his own kicks without sharing them with old gentlemen rapidly approaching retirement.

Ten minutes later he summoned Honeybody. It was one of Hawker's quirks that he professed not to remember the stout Sergeant's surname, referring to him as "um".

"Um," said Hawker abruptly, "how is it going?"

"Not so much going as waiting and sweating, sir."

(Doesn't know which way to jump, the old spider, surmised the Sergeant, smirking blandly in a way which he knew annoyed the Superintendent.)

Hawker mixed a glass of the effervescent salts, purchased in wholesale quantities, he took in summer for the wind which as the years lengthened became virtually the only feeling around his heart.

"The files show that Mr James has been submitting complete reports, save on this one matter, to the Greymouth Police. That is good because, as you know, it is not unnatural for the locals to like to wipe the Yard's eye with a rabbit-out-of-the-bag act. This way, with all cards, well nearly all, on the table, we take the wiper out of their hands, at least I hope so. This Lady Joanna Lambone Pye bit, now," his voice abruptly grew hard.

"She comes up once or twice a month to spend the night with this man who works in Covent Garden, one Ted Gould by name. A big raw-boned feller, worked in fruit and vegies since fifteen. A good run-of-the-mill chap is the market's summing up. Probably returns two thousand five hundred per year but actually takes home that much. He's a working partner in a syndicate handling the Spanish imports in season, but actually anything that turns up. Nothing against the firm, which is as honest as you can be in the fruit and veg. Gould himself has a funny sort of temper, vindictive is the word for it. A hail-well-met sort of fellow on surface, but if you get the wrong side of him he'll harbour a grudge. A bit of a fist fighter in his youth—Teddy boys was the popular name then, if you remember, Victorian clobber and a bicycle chain for your fun and games. Not that this means much. Most of them are now worrying about *their* children and the mortgage on the house. But Gould's rep. has stuck to him: his drinking mates watch their tongues a bit. He is a great motorist, by the way. Saturday and Sunday he likes to be on the road. A kind of restlessness, the point being that he probably knows Greymouth quite well as it is more or less a focal point for a good week-end run. I asked the locals to check whether he is known at the hotels there. No reply as yet. To sum up, he's a fairly predictable type of man. Likes his grog, but in moderation. A Scotch drinker but not a heavy one, by all accounts. A bit of a womaniser and the Lady Joanna is the high spot of his career. He boasts about sleeping with the peerage and not life ones neither. Doubtless he bows before climbing into the cot."

"Stick to the point," said Hawker, smothering a relieving belch.

"The point is that I have an identification that Lady Joanna arrived at his little flat off Charing Cross Road at seven o'clock in the evening. A man who sells cars remembers her saying 'good evening'. He'd sold a frightful crate that afternoon for double the real asking price so it is stuck in his mind. He was bold enough to ask her into his flat for a drink but she graciously refused. 'A rill lady'," mimicked the Sergeant. "Then there is a young bride who had her first quarrel—she'd mucked up the washing machine by dropping a fork into it. She'd flounced out, weeping, and went smack into her ladyship, who gave quiet words of comfort and told her to get back in, make her face up and look glamorous."

Hawker gave a windy sigh. "Is that in character? I had her down as a haughty upper-class, inbred, damn the peasants sort of lady."

"I'd say that Gould would be good in bed," said the Sergeant, irrelevantly. "As far as Lady Chatterley can love the gamekeeper she does—remember the case we brought when it was all explained in Court? I suppose our Lady might have been humming cheerfully to herself, loving the prolies as she thought of the delicate treats that night would bring."

"Keep to the point."

"The other point is that nobody saw Ted Gould. He left work at four o'clock, having been 'on' since three a.m., the partners taking the early shift in turns. I think he had the usual lunch at the 'Round House' as is his custom. Then comes a blank. He runs a three-year-old Triumph, in good order but not the sort of car you notice. Suppose that Lady Joanna, with a key, marched into his flat, attracting some attention on the way, while her lover nicked down to Greymouth and did the job?"

"Motive?"

Honeybody gave a massive shrug. "Money perhaps. Snape was a cruel man who liked tweaking people by their ears. Lady Joanna considered him a peasant so perhaps it was the case of 'Who will rid me of this damned solicitor?' Good knight Gould might have mounted his Triumph and ridden forth."

"You have sent a report to Greymouth?"

"I send a copy of all the routine stuff to headquarters there. Only the confidential stuff is phoned direct to Chief Inspector James."

"How long before you prove or disprove Mr James' theory?"

"Say two days. I can't hurry them. It's a massive piece of routine."

"And costly." Hawker thought sourly of the auditing department.

Honeybody thought of the harmless chores which lay ahead before opening time. All in all, it was a good assignment. He reported and accounted to nobody except the Chief Inspector and that by telephone. His periodical interviews with Hawker he did not count.

"In any case," he said, "the locals are not on Mr James' back."

In this he was wrong. The Chief Inspector had attended to routine matters, tidied up the Penelope Fennel file and delivered it with his own précis to a grateful Sir Charles.

That morning he had finished eggs and bacon, shared with Amanda, and was putting on his shoes when the Chief Constable rang through. His manner was far from warm as he requested Harry's presence at his office forthwith.

Something was up, thought the Chief Inspector a quarter of an hour later. The local Superintendent looked slyly triumphant and also present, perfectly assured, was Mr James Cold.

"The Super was not quite satisfied with Mr Cold's story," said the Chief. "When pressed Mr Cold admits that he omitted to say that at nine thirty p.m., through the crack in the door, he saw a pair of tan brogue shoes and grey socks pass towards the outer door into the alley. He thinks the trousers were a light grey. The man was walking softly."

"That was all he saw?" asked Harry, sceptically.

"The man's feet were very big, sir," said James Cold amicably. "My dad takes eleven and I reckon they were that."

"So he took big steps?"

"I think he must have, sir, with those big feet."

"And you saw both feet?"

Cold hesitated. "Only one, sir, as he put it down smack outside the crack I'd left in the door. There was a twenty-five watt globe in the passage, sir, enough to enable me to swear to the colour and type of shoe."

"Any more questions?" asked the Super, a bit sardonically.

Harry shook his head.

"All right, Mr Cold, you can go."

When the door had closed, Harry said: "He must have seen two feet, one passing the other, unless the man was in some way hopping."

The Super flushed angrily. "I went out there and got

down with the door open a crack. Visibility is clear but with very limited range."

"Dependent on how much the door was open."

"He said a crack. I opened it a quarter of an inch."

"If he persisted in saying he only saw one foot in court defence counsel would laugh him out of it," said Harry.

"I dare say the boy is a bit confused," said the Chief, "and these things can be smoothed out later. What we have to narrow down is suspects with large feet. His father, Cappy Cold, is out. He let us look through his house. The only shoes he owns are three pairs of orthopaedic ones, his feet having been pretty mashed up after all those years of football. Lady Joanna's, ah, paramour . . ." (only the working class had lovers, ruminated Harry) . . . "seems to be a big man."

"A raw-boned type," said the Chief Inspector, "with very big hands. I did not notice his feet. I'll soon find out."

"I thought of running up to town to see him," said the Super, too casually. Technically it was none of his business to do so.

However Harry smiled gracefully and said: "I'll tell Sergeant Honeybody to expect you. Meanwhile I had better see Lady Joanna and maybe get shown the door."

"Don't know what is coming over these girls," said the Chief. "The Lambone Pyes have always been respectable although the last Baron was a fool about money. I think these mini skirts affect the morals, I do really. Keep them well covered up and they're virtuous, as the Arabs very sensibly do." He sounded a bit wistful. Harry remembered that the Colonel's lady was indeed well covered up, even to shawls in the evening.

"I'd better be getting along," he said as he got up.

When he had gone, the Chief sat with bowed head peering into his empty coffee-cup for a long minute. "Super," he said, "I think that young man is taking it far too calmly. He must have something up his sleeve."

"Perhaps his brains, because he does not carry them within his skull, Colonel."

"You know his record?"

"The luckiest man who ever got out of uniform, they say. Besides, everybody knows that old Hawker uses him like a marionette."

"Hm. He did have something about young Cold having to see *two* feet."

"I haven't taken his deposition yet," the Super allowed himself a sly smile, "it'll cover any contingency by the time we're done. Well, I'll be getting the ten o'clock train, sir. I'll phone you directly I have news. Shouldn't take more than a couple of hours."

Worriedly the Colonel watched him go.

Rather to his surprise, Harry was admitted to Lady Joanna's presence as a matter of course. She was seated in her sun-trap of a room: a dictation machine was before her on the desk. She was cold, polite and impersonal. Her rat-trap lips opened and she said: "I had you in, Chief Inspector, because I preferred not to have a scene in front of my servants. However, from the Inquest proceedings you know very well who my legal people are. Why not badger them?"

Harry stood and looked at her for a minute. "Ted Gould is being interrogated concerning Snape's death."

Her face remained impassive.

"Have you no comment?" he said after a minute.

"Mr, um, James is it not? I care to say nothing. If you

manage to put me upon oath, I shall say something, of course, but you will have to do exactly that, I am afraid."

"You surely cannot allow an innocent man to remain in jeopardy?" The Chief Inspector had the uneasy feeling that, in the gloomy days before the welfare state had abolished such an expedient, Lady Joanna would have allowed him to be hanged.

"I have no statement to make." The thin lips tightened. Harry snapped his note-book shut with a sigh. He shook his head. "One would expect a lady of your position to co-operate with the police. After all, if the peerage will not support the Establishment, why is Bill Bloggs obligated to the the same?"

It stung her.

"There are certain areas of one's life one prefers not to make a matter of public knowledge."

He bowed and said he would let himself out.

As he drove home he came to the professional opinion that it would be impossible for the prosecution to call Lady Joanna if she refused to make any statement and once again regretted that England did not have an institution such as the American grand jury.

He parked the car as near to the police headquarters as he could get.

"Can I have a word with you, guv'nor?"

He thought he had seen him before, but perhaps he was merely a type. Tall, cadaverous, in his early twenties, with a great nose in a white face, long greasy side-burns and a blue suit with grease spots.

"Why not."

"Is it true that you chaps pay for info. received?" The young man spoke with more confidence, even a touch of bravado.

"We sometimes do. Of course, you've a duty as a citizen."

"Come off it! It's about Cold . . . the young one, James."

"I'd run to two quid, not more," said Harry casually.

"Well, James is in the money."

It was one of those moments that Harry wished he had not given up smoking: a cigarette lighted slowly afforded you time to think.

"How do you know?"

"He's buying into the Sigh."

"The what?"

"A coffee and spaghetti joint plus records. Groovy. The bloke what runs it wants to expand so Cold puts up two thousand nicker for a third interest. I happened to overhear them talking."

A born eavesdropper, thought the Chief Inspector as he got out his wallet.

The informer shambled away while Harry went to find an elderly and friendly police constable and invite him for a pint.

"The Sigh," said the constable, sipping, "only it's spelled Psi by the monster who runs it." He chuckled. "The reddest man—there is some doubt about the sex—you ever saw, face, hands, hair and politics. The place has been growing: good coffee and snacks at the right price and the kind of lighting and discs the kids go for. No harm: a hell of a lot of conversation which they may or not really understand. No hard drugs, although a certain amount of pot changes hands. Nothing illegal is consumed on premises. And young James Cold is taking a partnership, eh? He could do worse."

"It's just that I wondered where he got the money."

The constable massaged a blue jaw. "Now that is strange. His pa, old Cappy, has always spent the pay packet by

Thursday. You could mortgage his house—given him by the Supporters' Club it was—for two thousand easy, although it needs repairs. But I know the old man well, and mortgage his house is something he wouldn't do. Many a time I've heard him say that whatever happens he'll have his own roof over his head."

Harry thanked him, found out directions, and went to the Psi, multi-coloured on its façade, once a double-fronted lock-up shop. It smelled of a good Italian sauce and coffee. At a quarter to one it was filled. Nobody was listening to anybody else, so it seemed, and he was not noticed. The proprietor, as gross as the constable indicated, sweated in a tiny glass-fronted galley. Two smart young girls attended to the espresso machine and serving. It was the sort of place where you took your own food back from the counter. He stood there hesitating. Hardly looking up, a fat girl wriggled her bulk slightly along a kind of divan behind a narrow wooden bench-type table and said: "Here's a seat, dear."

Caught in a trap, the Chief Inspector purchased a small coffee and sat down, with some difficulty and embarrassment as the consequent pressure rucked up the fat girl's mini skirt to levels which he thought might result in an unpleasant chill. But could one pull it down in a friendly fashion? He was pondering the matter, when he saw she was looking at him with big eyes fairly ringed with mascara so that she looked like a panda.

"You're the nice head police aren't you?"

He must have boggled a bit, for she said: "I'm great friends with Jane Smithers. She said you were a worried, mousy, nice little fellow. I mean you don't *mind*, do you? I believe in speaking out, don't you?"

"I don't mind," he said, weakly.

"Jane isn't here because of the talk," she said, "and that

creature James Cold hasn't got the nerve. Jane's got friends who wouldn't mind giving him a one over the eye. Ruining a girl's reputation in a Police Court."

"Coroner's Court. And her name wasn't mentioned."

"Same thing, and everybody knew her name on account of going with that little creep."

Was there not a shade of envy in her voice?

"I hear that Master Cold is an owner here now," he said warily.

"You do get on to things quick. The rumour was only around this morning. Where did he get the money, dear, that's what we would all like to know."

"Savings perhaps."

"He never saved."

The Chief Inspector finished his coffee and excused himself. He walked along the street bent shouldered, in thought, so much so that he did not see young Mr James Cold pass him a few yards from the shop or notice the quick alarm upon his face.

It was no good phoning Honeybody at that time of day, so he went and ate a fretful lunch. In the afternoon he deliberately refrained from trying to speak to the Sergeant and set about the task of checking first mortgages. Unless of very recent date, Cappy Cold—his name proved to be Septimus Albert—had given no lien upon his property. He telephoned Elizabeth and told her he might be late, gaining his room at six thirty, only to find the inevitable memorandum asking whether he would attend Colonel Angel. He hoped to God this did not presage an offer of dinner. In fact it did not: the Colonel played it distinctly cool, Harry's white-haired-boy days being very much over in that quarter.

"I have here," the Colonel tapped a wad of papers, "the transcript of the Super's six p.m. incoming call. He will stay in London another day. He may have something. But what of Lady Joanna?"

"Refuses to comment. We would have grave difficulty in calling her to the stand. I think she will not admit a liaison with a common sort of man."

"Or commit perjury, have you thought of that, plus a before and after charge, even conspiracy. She certainly arrived at the Gould flat about six that evening. The Super checked and rechecked. But nobody saw Gould since just after lunch. And there was a man who had planned to call on him that night: they used to have a few drinks and watch TV. Both old school friends and in the same trade. He phoned the friend saying he was sorry but he had to go down to the country."

The Chief Inspector wished he had a stiff drink. "A white lie," he said. "He could hardly have a guest when in bed with the peerage. Any story would do."

"I think we will get him in," said the Chief Constable, "and try to break him, but first I am going to have every pub, policeman, filling station and parking attendant in Greymouth and *en route* questioned. He used a credit card for his petrol, the Super established, and we got a photograph taken by concealed camera."

"One thing which has come up is something about the younger Cold." The Chief Inspector recapitulated and the Chief Constable put on his dismal face.

"Are you saying that the murderer has bribed Cold?"

"Unless there is some other explanation why this young man, ostensibly without means other than his weekly earnings of—I checked this—twelve pounds and four shillings before tax, could raise two thousand pounds, it would seem to be."

"So Gould bribed him."

"The size eleven brogue shoe rules this out. Gould has a very large foot. If he wanted to tamper with evidence, surely he would specify a slim size eight or something to that effect?"

"It might be the Clever Gambit."

This was a trade term for a criminal who deliberately manufactures evidence against himself, courts arrest and is thus able to blow the prosecution sky high in court, relying on the fact that a verdict of "not guilty" precludes any further trial. It is risky, but a number of the cleverer criminals practise it.

"The detective novels wake the amateurs as well as professionals up to the clever hanky-panky," fairly groaned the Chief.

"Did the Superintendent talk to Gould himself?" asked Harry.

"No, he thought better not until tomorrow."

"I'd advise him to do it tonight. Also we should check on whether Lady Joanna remains at home or hies to London. The local constable would be the best bet on that. Send him round to ask about suspicious characters hanging around. If you authorise it, I'll phone now."

"Please do."

"She's at home," said the constable in his slowish voice. "I dropped in to see the gardener—complaints about the boys throwing stones at the greenhouse"—more likely a quart of ale in the potting-shed, thought Harry—"and he said her ladyship was in. That was half an hour ago."

"Keep checking every hour. If she sees you, act stupid and give her a talk about juvenile delinquents in the area. But if she leaves telephone headquarters."

"I'll do that, sir. I shan't see her, me going in the servants' gate and being on particularly friendly terms with the staff."

"Amazing how everybody knows about other people's business," grumbled the Chief. "Perhaps you'll hang on until his first report at least."

Thus it was that three hours later the Chief Inspector had finished dining with the Chief Constable at his Club, an excellent meal ruined by the necessity of fabricating excuses to prevent a following session of chess. If not completely thawed, Colonel Angel was at least hedging his bet. Shortly after eleven two phone calls were relayed, the first from the constable watching Lady Joanna Lambone Pye. By means into which Harry was too tired to pry, the constable had ascertained that at ten o'clock her ladyship had bathed, imbibed two very dry kümmels, taken a popular and fairly harmless sleeping pill, and gone to bed in a flaming temper. He did not put it past the constable to gawp through windows, but it was probably a garrulous lady's maid hypnotised by the P.C.'s bucolic charms.

"Pity," said the Chief Constable.

At eleven thirty, when Harry's head had started to ache— the Chief had decided views on Rhodesia—the Super came through. When he returned from what his slightly nineteen-twentyish turn of phrase called "the blower" the Chief Constable was groaning. "This damned fellow Gould told the Super to eff off. He let him into the flat quite politely— Super says he had drink taken—listened without comment and then closed up. There was nothing to be done. I sometimes get an insight into the minds of blokes who use torture, I'm sure. Nothing the Super could do but depart."

"I'd settle for a sensible wire-tapping policy," said Harry who had decided views on the matter, "given that impossibility, a politician with guts. Your Mr Gould was probably on the wire to Lady Joanna as soon as the Super's backside was through the back door."

"We'll know," said the Chief, "because that local constable sleeps with her cook. Oh, he's a bachelor so I've never troubled to have him on the carpet."

"A female cook?"

"Good God, yes, we are a heterosexual force down here, though one understands that off Victoria Street it may be different."

"We're all too old."

"And the Lambone Pye family have always had female cooks. Sensible thing—they do not get on the grog quite so much and are better at pastry."

At one a.m. devious shiftings—an imaginary cold on the part of Amanda being the most powerful—got Harry off the hook and the Chief Constable dropped him off near the Cottage.

"I wish the hell he'd go to bed," mourned the Chief Inspector to his wife who had.

"He is unique," she decided. "It is so refreshing to meet a man who doesn't."

"Anything from Honeybody?"

"A cryptic message," she said, "him being a bit full at eleven o'clock. He said that he thought things were going to be all right. Then he started to sing and I cut off, which reminds me, Lady Fennel rang. Have you heard of the Clarence J. Boddingham Foundation?"

Harry groaned.

"It's highly cultural," Elizabeth intoned the sacred words with appropriate reverence. "Like Americans are. You don't find bra manufacturers here leaving all that money to Higher Things."

"I didn't much think there was anything higher," said Harry, hanging up his trousers.

"Now do not be trying, please. I have had a hard day.

They have found a hitherto unsuspected rich load of folk music, possibly of Anglo-Saxon origin, in Greymouth, complete with strange stringed instruments which might be of Arab origin. The American team, though partly coloured, have been very d. about it, to the point of suggesting that Lady F. be allowed to participate to the extent of founding a small associated institute here. She apparently has a hundred thousand dollars which she does not know what to do with. One of the nice Americans will advise her."

"When is all this going to happen?"

"She will announce it at the Grey Goat tomorrow night."

"God Almighty!" The Chief Inspector sat on the end of the bed.

"It has a long history of what the chief American, who calls himself Billy the Song, styles cultural participation in depth at the community level, by which he means the Grey Goat has been the scene of working class booze-ups for four hundred odd years. The name may have some witchcraft association, you know, or a pagan base. Anyway Lady F. thinks it is fitting to get right back to the grass roots, as she expresses it. There are a very old couple called Tubb who will sing and dance anciently before Lady Fennel announces her endowment of a Greymouth Branch of the Foundation. Everyone will be there. It is at nine thirty and wear your new grey suit, not one of those baggy things. I am so glad Honeybody is not here. We could hardly have kept him away when he heard that Lady F. is turning on unlimited grog."

The Chief Inspector got his dressing-gown and padded away to the bathroom.

IX

THE THOUGHT OF Lady Fennel's bank book had prodded the landlord of the Grey Goat to great heights, thought Harry, who arrived at eight thirty next evening, his wife having grandly arranged to make her entrance with the Fennels. The Inquest Room had been scoured and the smell of a couple of hundred years of cigar smoke and cabbage water—only the cabbages now being much in evidence—temporarily chased out of the window. Police instinct caused Harry to prowl "out the back", to discover the landlord and four sullen temporary waiters tying paper napkins round bottles of champagne cider. Harry dealt peremptorily with the landlord: these days at a certain stage they always rang in the cider and there was really no law against it.

"Never mind that," he said sharply, "but what should I eat?"

"For Chris' sake don't get on to the prawns," gasped one stertorous old waiter.

"The mutton pies, sir, are superb," said the landlord, attempting a bow, the effect being ruined as he was kneeling down, "and the game pàté. Just avoid the prawns and the salmon suprême and I take my oath you'll do fabulously. And Henry here will see you do right well on the Moët and Chandon. It does not do, sir, to give the great things of life to the lower classes, we find. They either get obstreperous or right randy. A good draught of cider merely cools the blood, so we find in the catering, and the ladies are grateful for it."

The Chief Inspector was in no mood for company, and going back mooched over a warm light ale. Honeybody had been phoning at intervals all day. It was the time of the kill, which always induced in him a mixture of sheer sexual excitement, nervous dyspepsia and a tendency to get drunk on very little. Hawker had agreed that the matter had best not be discussed with the local police: the local Superintendent had probably got on the aged toes at the Yard, thought Harry, always a mistake, as the other extremity possessed vicious teeth, albeit false.

Colonel Angel, the Chief Constable, had been toey, probably from a policeman's instinct that "something was up". Harry had gone through the motions of seeing James Cold during his lunch hour and the youth had talked about his rights, demanded a free solicitor, and declared that his father's life savings were invested in the coffee bar. He was also about to become a married man, the happy girl being one Jane Smithers.

"You've read that bit about a wife not being able to be forced to give evidence against her husband," Harry had said.

James Cold had sat without replying, but with interest in his tiny eyes.

"It's not quite true," said the Chief Inspector. "A lifetime of wedlock against what a clever lawyer can do! Remember that, my fine friend. And a wife costs around eight quid a week after tax. If somebody has given you, say, three thousand to stop your trap, it means roughly six years of the kind of bliss you've been getting for fish, chip and cinema money. When that's gone, you've got the ball and chain and maybe three little ones eating their ruddy heads off."

"She's a good worker," said Cold, "and she'll be behind the espresso machine."

"That's what you think. Suppose you find out what she spends on her hair, let alone what they clutter up the bathroom with. 'Gentle Dew' at two quid a bottle I found my old lady with only last week. Takes out the wrinkles. You'd save yourself a lot of trouble by a quiet chat."

It had come to nought. He would, Harry thought with a certain relish which he despised in himself, have Master Cold blubbering in the witness box before he was done with him.

"Hallo there, my dear sir. I thought I saw your horse and cart in the parking lot."

With an inward wince, the Chief Inspector recognised Ralf—with an F—Fennel.

"A lovely job you did, so Charles is saying, on rehabilitating old Penelope. Almost makes me wish you were right."

Harry bought a double Scotch. "You think she was guilty?"

"Women always are," said Ralf. "Nothing easier than to poison a man. 'Your favourite dish, my love, tonight.'"

"It is more difficult to get rid of wives," admitted Harry from experience. "Throwing them down a flight of stairs is generally best, but the back-room boys nearly always pinpoint that."

"Did you hear of the pyjama-girl case back in Sydney? The girl they had pickled in formalin up at the University? It was like this...."

Half an hour later, Harry supposed they might as well go up. They used the interior stairs, the visiting gentry being ushered up the back stairs, used by the Coroner on less festive occasions.

Either they were late or people were early, after all it is not every day that a small country town finds itself the repository of a rich seam of medieval culture. Sir Charles Fennel was standing, stout and florid, towering over his fellows in one corner. Drinks and canapés were being served. The Chief Inspector settled for a greasy sausage roll with the sterile taste of sawdust about it. The official greeter, big, black and charming, was Billy the Song. "There's my good secretary over there, knowing nobody," Ralf Fennel excused himself abruptly.

With Elizabeth as a kind of lady-in-waiting, Lady Fennel made her entrance. She was superbly dressed and altogether the Chief Inspector was not displeased to see his wife, over-topping her ladyship by five inches, behaving so creditably in this production number, though recoiling at the thought that it was costing two baby-sitters and a half-witted youth with a strange affinity for dogs, who loved him on sight, to cope with Mr Bones.

Billy the Song greeted as effusively as a thirty-thousand-pound endowment (with hints of more to come) deserved. It was proper, he observed, that the good folk of Greymouth should share in the goodies hitherto reserved for the Clarence J. Boddingham Foundation. "And now, we shall continue the refreshments while these local worthies, Mr and Mrs Tubb, *the* Tubbs as they are destined to be known, will sing and caper something we think dates from Edward the Second."

"And he came to a very funny end," said Ralf Fennel, behind Harry.

"Destiny shaped *his* end all right," agreed the Chief Inspector.

Ignoring the soothing voice of Billy the Song, Harry noted that the Chuck family were on the dais ordinarily occupied by the Coroner. Professor Chuck had what was probably a lute: his brother Paul, the antiquary, was preparing to puff into a kind of serpentine tube, while Miss Charlotte Chuck, unwisely clad in floppy white trousers, held a stringed instrument. The Tubbs made their ancient way forward: the Chucks commenced a collective wheezing and the old people started to caper. Tubb, exhaling whisky fumes as he skipped past the Chief Inspector, was extraordinarily nimble. Whatever embrocation he used was very efficacious, or perhaps in these days it was penicillin or K.H.3. Mrs Tubb, who was doing the singing, verged a trifle on the apopleptic side as her plump cheeks throbbed, intoning in a hoarse voice:

"Dingling, dingly, upsee zithy
Parsley pardon ee besom."

"It was when they brought the ewes down from the hills at the end of summer," confided one of the American team in the interval between verses, "decked out in juniper branches and scraps of dyed woollen material."

The Tubbs did two more numbers before being led away for restoration by the publican. They were succeeded by two hefty maidens who did an involved straddle-legged dance. ("Of incalculable antiquity," said the commentator, while Miss Charlotte Chuck was threatened by a fit of violent coughing into her handkerchief.)

Now the Tubbs were back, but this time behind them loomed the immense girth of Sergeant Honeybody, the tall dyspeptic Superintendent Hawker by his side.

There was a strange silence, one of the many the old Court must have sustained.

"Ralf Fennel, alias George Brighton," said the old Superintendent, head poised for any alert photographer, "I must ask you to accompany me as I have reason to believe that you can help me into enquiries touching the death of one Gerald Snape."

Ralf stood there saying nothing, eyes restlessly devouring the room. Honeybody moved close to him.

"Take it easy," said the Superintendent. "There is no need at all to say anything here. And now," his cold eyes flicked sideways to Ralf's secretary—once you knew, thought Harry, the consanguinity was unmistakable. "I must ask you, Miss Brighton, to accompany me on the same errand." He touched her arm very lightly.

The Chief Inspector moved in behind the four of them as they moved off towards the back stairs, although he knew that four other men and two police cars were at the entrance, but Hawker waved him away, obviously wanting nobody to share this moment of choice publicity. The old man would have seen that the Press were duly tipped off: not only because of his own desire for publicity, important to a man for whom retirement or a nice Government sinecure loomed, but for the fact that publicity usually weighed heavily against an accused person. This fact the Chief Inspector, like other policemen, accepted because it went some way to counter-balance Judges' Rules, themselves so heavily weighted in favour of an ingenious criminal.

Harry saw that Billy the Song, old battler that he was, was sweating blood.

"Now, ladies and gentlemen, in this day and age nobody is shocked by fertility rites. In the reign of Elizabeth the First, the average expectation of life was twenty-seven years, so adults in fact were younger, and as a right proper Englishman would say, thus nippier on their pins"—general laughter, but a worried frown from Sir Charles Fennel. "Mr and Mrs Tubb—and I don't know how they do it at their age"—embarrassed titters—"will now . . ."

But Harry was creeping down the back stairs and two hours later was in bed, having dismissed baby and dog sitters, drinking whisky and milk when his wife entered.

"You did your best to mess up poor Lady Fennel's do, you monster. Can't you arrest people at church or something? Sir Charles is worried and wants to see you."

"For your ears alone, my love..." The Chief Inspector had to talk for an hour before he was mercifully allowed to put the light out.

Six days later the first groan of the wheels of justice had been completed. George Brighton and his second cousin, Irene Brighton, had been committed by a Bench consisting of a senile ex-grocer appointed for past services in the Conservative interest, a vast lady who bullied the local Women's Institutes, and a nervous retired builder, to stand their trial at the next Assizes, where their fate would rest upon twelve similar persons. Elizabeth, the children and the dog had been removed—at Government expense—to London and Harry, Honeybody and Superintendent Hawker had taken rooms at the Grey Goat. It was Thursday and, having wrung every penny they could from the permitted expense accounts, they were about to pack up to leave the following day.

"Telephone, Chief Inspector." The landlord was most respectful. One of the things about such provincial forays was that once an arrest had been made one became a famous, albeit overnight identity and it was a pleasure to be goggled at by teenage ladies with well developed parts, bowed to by aldermen, and toadied to by tradesmen.

"Fennel here, old man." Sir Charles had unbent so that one almost heard his corsets groan. "Understand that the good lady has returned. M' wife asked her—you of course included—to spend a long week-end when possible. Could you have a bite tonight at sevenish? Informal, y' know."

Harry said he would be delighted but consulted Hawker, who was struggling with the new elastic-sided boots issued free to senior officers with varicose veins.

"It won't do us any political harm with the Conservatives," said the aged Superintendent, waggling a shoe horn, "because Fennel is always good for ten thousand quid come election time and we get more and more political interference every day."

Sir Charles handsomely sent his car along at six thirty. There were only the three of them and host and hostess restrained open curiosity until the brandy.

"It began when Snape was going through your family papers," said Harry, "and the fact was apparent the Fennels are and were large-boned, fair-headed, blue-eyed people. And the self-styled Ralf was dark and small-boned. Snape was a man who loved a secret. He hugged this one, but in fact he was wrong: the late Ralf was in fact small and dark, the genetic strain having altered. Ralf was a farmer from Grafton: George Brighton was a crook from the Melbourne slums. He did two short terms inside, for obtaining goods on false pretences, but he was nobody's fool and knew a lot about the food industry, in which he sometimes got a job, being a trained butcher. Both men were twenty-seven years old in 1939 when they joined up. Things were getting rather too hot for George Brighton and the Army seemed a way to lie low.

"In 1940 they became prisoners-of-war of the Italians,

ending up in a camp in Germany. That is where they met, both Sergeants, and became friends, great friends. No doubt Brighton came to know Ralf's life story as well as his own as the boring months trickled by, plus the existence of a wealthy English branch. Shortly before the end came the camp was bombed by error and Ralf was killed. Brighton was repatriated to Eastbourne, drew out his back pay and simply disappeared, just walked out one fine day and vanished. We know what happened: he turned up here and your father gave him a job."

"Ralf was never all-of-one-piece," said Lady Fennel. "That rather ridiculous brand of conversation punctuated by moments of great shrewdness: and he was first class in business, Charles says."

"First rate," said her husband, "very useful as far as he went. I do not suppose it is evidence," he added ruefully, "but my accountants, after two days of overtime, believe that he was setting the business up for a killing. He had taken nothing yet, but certain financial alterations had been made which make it look as though he could have been planning to transfer, say a quarter of a million, into fake companies of his own."

"He was bored with it," said the Chief Inspector, "besides which his second cousin Irene Brighton had turned up. She is giving evidence for the Crown. It is either that or fifteen years for her. Crooks never lose touch with each other completely, and Irene was a very successful lady confidence trickster back in Australia. When he planned his coup, he brought her over because he could not afford to have a stranger with access to the private files.

"You were quite right in seeing that his personality did not quite jell, Lady Fennel. A long-term confidence trick is too difficult to play by half. Usually it is a matter of a quick, skilled impersonation but over the years Brighton slipped sometimes."

"Was he not taking a risk?" grunted Sir Charles.

"Only the remote one that an old acquaintance should turn up at Greymouth, and he might be able to bluff it out or to pay hush money."

"He never wanted to travel," said Fennel. "I wanted him to go to Australia once. I thought he hedged a bit."

"Hedged a bit?"

"Well, he produced a variety of reasons: too many. Actually I merely thought he might have some unpleasant memories. I was a fool. In business I find that if a man does not want to do a reasonable thing it saves you money to find out why."

"Actually Victorian districts tended to slip into Ralf's conversation. And ostensibly he came from New South Wales. His conversation was a little knowing, too. The word Collingwood was on Snape's scratch-pad. It was the name of a local pub, but it was also at one time a suburb of Melbourne which produced violent criminals. Snape had written to an Australian firm of solicitors asking for the name of a reliable investigator. He was fool enough to bait Brighton. 'Oh, how long since you saw Collingwood, Ralf?' My own presence in the area did not lead to Brighton's ease of mind: after all I was sort of investigating the family. He went to see Snape about a legitimate enquiry, hid in one of the old rooms, and returned after the staff had left. Snape used to wait with the alley door open certain days a week in case any of his money-lending clients turned up. That was a risk that Brighton had to take and not too large a one. Let us imagine he held the knife—which is not identified—behind his back and whipped open the door of Snape's office. By the time Snape said, 'What is this about?' he'd be dead.

Ever noticed that for a small man Ralf had muscles? He was an amateur wrestler.

"The presence of young James Cold and his girl gave him a shock, but he sat it out. He heard them come in. What did strike me is that his secretary alibied him until ten thirty, the only one of Snape's visitors who had such a cast-iron one. We always tap around cast-iron alibis pretty hard. Of course he had to embellish it all: we find murderers do, they cannot sit pat and sweat it out. In this case he approached James Cold and gave him—we think it was three thousand in notes to say he had seen a pair of enormous feet walk past. He made up a plausible story. I naturally thought of who had small feet. Then it was a matter of endless cables and phone calls to Aussie, about two thousand it cost with the Australian labour. I waited here."

"I suppose he'll get life," said Sir Charles.

"He just might get off," said the Chief Inspector. "I suppose you would prefer charges of impersonation?"

"And expose my father and myself as fools?"

"I thought not. As we have it now, young Cold is not talking, nor is old Cappy Cold. Counsel is not sure how we could put him in the box for the prosecution, and the defence won't. Irene Brighton's evidence is disastrous, but not conclusive. She says she did not know the purpose of the alibi. And moreover Brighton had a head wound when he was captured. Records say he would have got a thirty per cent pension. We think he will plead diminished responsibility, lack of memory and manslaughter. In which case any reference to your family will largely be left out, or introduced casually. He may get off with five years."

Deliberately he started talking of something else. No good embellishing it by describing the manoeuvres of George

Brighton's most expensive legal advisers or the steps taken by the Treasury staff to circumvent them.

As he was going, Fennel, with slight embarrassment, gave him an envelope. "A slight token of our appreciation, old man."

Harry forced himself not to open it until he was getting into bed. It was for five hundred pounds.

Next morning Hawker departed in a bad temper and an official Humber. Harry and Sergeant Honeybody were in the rented car. It was a fine morning and the Chief Inspector experienced the balm of eased financial circumstances. Suddenly he stopped: outside the premises of Cryer, the carpenter, who, by his discovery of Penelope Fennel's diary, had started it all.

"I shall reward Elizabeth with a whatnot," he said.

"Eh?"

"A prime Victorian whatnot to wipe the eye of the lady next door. Half a mo'."

Amid the smell of turpentine the Cryers, for twenty pounds, found him a most hideous whatnot and carried it back to the car.

"What the hell did they do with it?" asked Honeybody.

"Nobody could possibly ascertain that: we are very careful to make them that way," grinned the carpenter as they stowed it in the back. "Here, I found this bottle when smashing up the last of the old wardrobe, since you were interested. It was kind of glued behind a joist."

It was not a large medicine bottle. Harry drove on a couple of hundred yards before stopping and getting out the emergency petrol tin. The grime and grease of a hundred years covered it and he sacrificed a handkerchief, working carefully.

The type on the label was faded orange: *Poison* it said. Underneath faded handwritten script noted: *Antimonial salt*.

"I had that feeling," said the Chief Inspector, "that she was guilty. The diary was a second line of defence. Perhaps too clever, they always are. She could not bear to share Captain Bradstreet with another woman, nor to see him steal her money. So..."

"What now?"

The Chief Inspector bent and slipped the little old bottle down a street drain.

"It doesn't matter now."

"No," said Honeybody, "but then it never does."